CROSSFIRE TRAIL

Fawcett Gold Medal Books
by Louis L'Amour:

CROSSFIRE TRAIL

HELLER WITH A GUN

HONDO

KILKENNY

LAST STAND AT PAPAGO WELLS

SHOWDOWN AT YELLOW BUTTE

THE TALL STRANGER

TO TAME A LAND

UTAH BLAINE

CROSSFIRE TRAIL

Louis L'Amour

A FAWCETT GOLD MEDAL BOOK • NEW YORK

CROSSFIRE TRAIL

All the characters in this book are fictitious, and any resemblance to actual persons living or dead is purely coincidental.

Copyright © 1954 by Ace Books, Inc.

Published by Fawcett Gold Medal Books, a unit of CBS Publications, the Consumer Publishing Division of CBS Inc.

ISBN: 0-449-13836-4

Printed in the United States of America

21 20 19 18 17 16 15 14 13 12

CROSSFIRE TRAIL

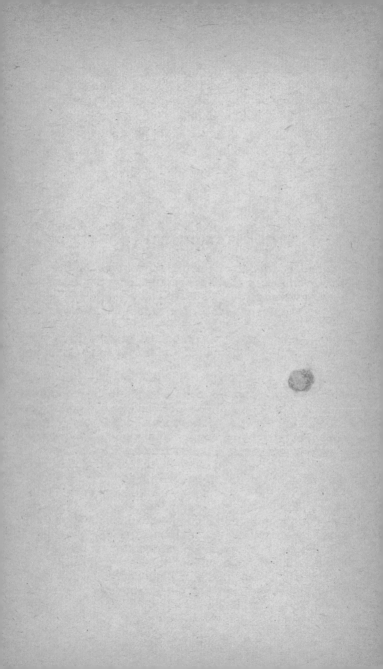

I

IN THE DANK, odorous fo'c'sle a big man with wide
shoulders sat at a scarred mess table, his feet spread
to brace himself against the roll of the ship. A brass
hurricane lantern, its light turned low, swung from a
beam overhead, and in the vague light the big man
studied a worn and sweat-stained chart.

There was no sound in the fo'c'sle but the distant
rustle of the bow wash about the hull, the lazy creak
of the square rigger's timbers, a few snores from sleep-
ing men, and the hoarse, rasping breath of a man who
was dying in the lower bunk.

The big man who bent over the chart wore a slip-
over jersey with alternate red and white stripes, a broad
leather belt with a brass buckle, and coarse jeans. On
his feet were woven leather sandals of soft, much-oiled
leather. His hair was shaggy and uncut, but he was
cleanshaven except for a mustache and burnsides.

The chart he studied showed the coast of northern
California. He marked a point on it with the tip of his
knife, then checked the time with a heavy gold watch.
After a swift calculation, he folded the chart and re-
placed it in an oilskin packet with other papers and
tucked the packet under his jersey, above his belt.

Rising, he stood for an instant, canting to the roll of
the ship, staring down at the white-haired man in the
lower bunk. There was something about the big man
that would make him stand out in any crowd. He was

a man born to command, not only because of his splendid physique and the strength of his character, but because of his personality.

He knelt beside the bunk and touched the dying man's wrist. The pulse was feeble, Rafe Caradec crouched there, waiting, watching, thinking.

In a few hours at most, possibly even in a few minutes, this man would die. In the long year at sea his health had broken down under forced labor and constant beatings, and this last one had broken him up internally. When Charles Rodney was dead he, Rafe Caradec, would do what he must.

The ship rolled slightly, and the older man sighed and his lids opened suddenly. For a moment he stared upward into the ill-smelling darkness, then his head turned. He saw the big man crouched beside him and he smiled. His hand fumbled for Rafe's.

"You—you've got the papers? You won't forget?"

"I won't forget."

"You must be careful."

"I know."

"See my wife, Carol. Explain to her that I didn't run away, that I wasn't afraid. Tell her I had the money, and was comin' back. I'm worried about the mortgage I paid. I don't trust Barkow."

The man lay silent, breathing deeply, hoarsely. For the first time in three days he was conscious and aware.

"Take care of 'em, Rafe," he said. "I've got to trust you! You're the only chance I have! Dyin' ain't bad except for them. And to think—a whole year has gone by. Anything may have happened!"

"You'd better rest," Rafe said gently.

"It's late, for that. He's done me in this time. Why did this happen to me, Rafe? To us?"

Caradec shrugged his powerful shoulders. "I don't know. No reason, I guess. We were just there at the wrong time. We took a drink we shouldn't have taken."

The old man's voice lowered. "You're goin' to try—tonight?"

Rafe smiled then. "Try? Tonight we're goin' ashore, Rodney. This is our only chance. I'm goin' to see the captain first."

Rodney smiled and lay back, his face a shade whiter, his breathing more gentle.

A year they had been together, a brutal, ugly, awful year of labor, blood, and bitterness. It had begun, that year, one night in San Francisco in Hongkong Bohl's place on the Barbary Coast. Rafe Caradec was just back from Central America with a pocket full of money, his latest revolution cleaned up, the proceeds in his pocket, and some of it in the bank.

The months just past had been jungle months, dripping jungle, fever-ridden and stifling with heat and humidity. It had been a period of raids and battles, but finally it was over, and Rafe had taken his payment in cash and moved on. He had been on the town, making up for lost time—Rafe Caradec, gambler, soldier of fortune, wanderer of the far places.

Somewhere along the route that night he had met Charles Rodney, a sun-browned cattleman who had come to Frisco to raise money for his ranch in Wyoming. They had had a couple of drinks and dropped in at Hongkong Bohl's dive. They'd had a drink there, too, and when they awakened it had been to the slow, long roll of the sea, and the brutal voice of Bully Borger, skipper of the *Mary S.*

Rafe had cursed himself for a tenderfoot and a fool. To have been shanghaied like any drunken farmer! He had shrugged it off, knowing the uselessness of resistance. After all, it was not his first trip to sea.

Rodney had been wild. He had rushed to the captain and demanded to be put ashore, and Bully Borger had knocked him down and booted him senseless while the mate stood by with a pistol. That had happened twice more until Rodney returned to work almost a

9

cripple, and frantic with worry over his wife and daughter.

As always, the crew had split into cliques. One of these consisted of Rafe, Rodney, Roy Penn, "Rock" Mullaney and "Tex" Brisco. Penn had been a law student and occasional prospector. Mullaney was an able-bodied seaman, hardrock miner and cowhand. They had been shanghaied in Frisco in the same lot with Rafe and Rodney. Tex Brisco was a Texas cowhand who had been shanghaied from a waterfront dive in Galveston where he had gone to look at the sea.

Finding a friend in Rafe, Rodney had told him the whole story of his coming to Wyoming with his wife and daughter. Of what drought and Indians had done to his herd, and how finally he had mortgaged his ranch to a man named Barkow.

Rustlers had invaded the country and he had lost cattle. Finally reaching the end of his rope, he had gone to San Francisco. Surprisingly, he had met Barkow and some others and paid off the mortgage. A few hours later, wandering into Hongkong Bohl's place which had been recommended to him by Barkow's friends, he had been doped, robbed, and shanghaied.

When the ship returned to Frisco after a year Rodney had demanded to be put ashore, and Borger had laughed at him. Then Charles Rodney had tackled the big man again, and that time the beating had been final. With Rodney dying, the *Mary S* had finished her loading and slipped out of port so he could be conveniently "lost at sea."

The cattleman's breathing had grown gentler, and Rafe leaned his head on the edge of the bunk, dozing.

Rodney had given him a deed to the ranch, a deed that gave him a half share, the other half belonging to Rodney's wife and daughter. Caradec had promised to save the ranch if he possibly could. Rodney had also given him Barkow's signed receipt for the money.

Rafe's head came up with a jerk. How long he had

slept he did not know, yet—he stiffened as he glanced at Charles Rodney. The hoarse, rasping breath was gone, the even, gentle breath was no more. Rodney was dead.

For an instant, Rafe held the old man's wrist, then drew the blanket over Rodney's face. Abruptly then, he got up. A quick glance at his watch told him they had only a few minutes until they would sight Cape Mendocino. Grabbing a small bag of things off the upper bunk, he turned quickly to the companionway.

Two big feet and two hairy ankles were visible on the top step. They moved, and step by step a man came down the ladder. He was a big man, bigger than Rafe, and his small, cruel eyes stared at him, then at Rodney's bunk.

"Dead?"

"Yes."

The big man rubbed a fist along his unshaven jowl. He grinned at Rafe.

"I heard him speak aboot the ranch. It could be a nice thing, that. I heerd aboot them ranches. Money in 'em." His eyes brightened with cupidity and cunning. "We share an' share alike, eh?"

"No." Caradec's voice was flat. "The deed is made out to his daughter and me. His wife is to share, also. I aim to keep nothin' for myself."

The big man chuckled hoarsely. "I can see that!" he said. "Josh Briggs is no fool, Caradec! You're intendin' to get it all for yourself. I want mine!" He leaned on the hand rail of the ladder. "We can have a nice thing, Caradec. They said there was trouble over there? Huh! I guess we can handle any trouble, an' make some ourselves."

"The Rodneys get it all," Rafe said. "Stand aside. I'm in a hurry."

Briggs' face was ugly. "Don't get high an' mighty with me!" he said roughly. "Unless you split even with

11

me, you don't get away. I know aboot the boat you've got ready. I can stop you there, or here."

Rafe Caradec knew the futility of words. There are some natures to whom only violence is an argument. His left hand shot up suddenly, his stiffened fingers and thumb making a V that caught Briggs where his jawbone joined his throat.

The blow was short, vicious, unexpected. Briggs' head jerked back and Rafe hooked short and hard with his right, then followed through with a smashing elbow that flattened Briggs' nose and showered him with blood.

Rafe dropped his bag, then struck left and right to the body, then left and right to the chin. The last two blows cracked like pistol shots. Josh Briggs hit the foot of the ladder in a heap, rolled over and lay still, his head partly under the table. Rafe picked up his bag and went up the ladder without so much as a backward glance.

On the dark deck Rafe Caradec moved aft along the starb'rd side. A shadow moved out from the mainm'st.

"You ready?"

"Ready, Rock."

Two more men got up from the darkness near the foot of the mast and all four hauled the boat from its place and got it to the side.

"This the right place?" Penn asked.

"Almost." Caradec straightened. "Get her ready. I'm going to call on the Old Man."

In the darkness he could feel their eyes on him. "You think that's wise?"

"No, but he killed Rodney. I've got to see him."

"You goin' to kill Borger?"

It was like them that they did not doubt he could if he wished. Somehow he had always impressed men so, that what he wanted to accomplish, he would accomplish.

"No, just a good beatin'. He's had it comin' for a long time."

Mullaney spat. He was a stocky, muscular man. "You cussed right he has! I'd like to help."

"No, there'll be no help for either of us. Stand by and watch for the mate."

Penn chuckled. "He's tied up aft, by the wheel."

Rafe Caradec turned and walked forward. His soft leather sandals made no noise on the hardwood deck, nor on the companionway as he descended. He moved like a shadow along the bulkhead, and saw the door of the captain's cabin standing open. He was inside and had taken two steps before the captain looked up.

Bully Borger was big, almost a giant. He had a red beard around his jaw bone under his chin. He squinted from cold, gray eyes at Rafe.

"What's wrong?" he demanded. "Trouble on deck?"

"No, Captain," Rafe said shortly, "there's trouble here. I've come to beat you within an inch of your life, Captain. Charles Rodney is dead. You ruined his life, Captain, and then you killed him."

Borger was on his feet, catlike. Somehow he had always known this moment would come. A dozen times he had told himself he should kill Caradec, but the man was a seaman, a first class, able-bodied seaman, and in the lot of shanghaied crews there were few. So he had delayed.

He lunged at the drawer for his brass knuckles.

Rafe had been waiting for that, poised on the balls of his feet. His left hand dropped to the captain's wrist and his right hand sank to the wrist in the captain's middle. It stopped Borger, that punch did. Stopped him flatfooted for only an instant, but that instant was enough. Rafe's head darted forward, butting the bigger man in the face, and Rafe felt the bones crunch under his hard skull.

Yet the agony gave Borger a burst of strength, and he tore the hand with the knucks loose and got his fingers through their holes. He lunged, swinging a roundhouse blow that would have dropped a bull elephant. Rafe went under the swing, his movements timed perfectly, his actions almost negligent. He smashed left and right to the middle, and the punches drove wind from Borger's stomach and he doubled up, gasping.

Rafe dropped a palm to the back of the man's head and shoved down, hard. At the same instant, his knee came up, smashing Borger's face into a gory pulp.

Bully Borger, the dirtiest fighter on many a waterfront, staggered back, moaning with pain. His face expressionless, Rafe Caradec stepped in and threw punches with both hands, driving, wicked punches that had the power of those broad shoulders behind them, and timed with the rolling of the ship. Left, right, left, right, blows that cut and chopped like meat cleavers. Borger tottered and fell back across the settee.

Rafe wheeled to see Penn's blond head in the doorway. Roy Penn stared at the bloody hulk, then at Rafe.

"Better come on. The Cape's showing off the starb'rd bow."

When they had the boat in the water they slid down the rope one after the other, then Rafe slashed it with his belt knife, and the boat dropped back. The black bulk of the ship swept by them. Her stern lifted, then sank and Rafe, at the tiller, turned the bow of the boat toward the monstrous blackness of the Cape.

Mullaney and Penn got the sail up when the mast was stepped, then Penn looked around at Rafe.

"That was mutiny, you know."

"It was," Rafe said calmly. "I didn't ask to go aboard, and knockout drops in a Barbary Coast dive ain't my way of askin' for a year's job!"

"A year?" Penn swore. "Two years and more, for me. For Tex, too."

"You know this coast?" Mullaney asked.

Rafe nodded. "Not well, but there's a place just north of the Cape where we can run in. To the south the sunken ledges and rocks might tear our bottom out, but I think we can make this other place."

The mountainous headland loomed black against the gray-turning sky of the hours before daybreak. The seaward face of the Cape was rocky and waterworn along the shoreline. Rafe, studying the currents and the rocks, brought the boat neatly in among them and headed for a boulder-strewn gray beach where water curled and left a white ruffle of surf.

They scrambled out of the boat and threw their gear on the narrow beach.

"How about the boat?" Texas demanded. "Do we leave it?"

"Shove her off, cut a hole in the bottom, and let her sink," Rafe said.

When the hole had been cut, they let the sea take the boat offshore a little, watching it fill and sink. Then they picked up their gear and Rafe Caradec led them inland, working along the shoulder of the mountain. The northern slope was covered with brush and trees, and afforded some concealment. Fog was rolling in from the sea, and soon the gray cottony shroud of it settled over the countryside.

When they had several miles behind them, Rafe drew to a halt. Penn opened the sack he was carrying and got out some bread, figs, coffee and a pot.

"Stole 'em out of the captain's stores," he said. "Figured we might as well eat."

"Got anything to drink?" Mullaney rubbed the dark stubble of his wide jaws.

"Uh-huh. Two bottles of rum. Good stuff from Jamaica."

"You'll do to ride the river with," Tex said, squatting on his heels. He glanced up at Rafe. "What comes now?"

"Wyomin' for me." Rafe broke some sticks and put them into the fire Rock was kindling. "I made my promise to Rodney, and I'll keep it."

"He trusted you."

"Yes. I'm not goin' to let him down. Anyway," he added, "Wyomin's a long way from here, and we should be as far away as we can get. They may try to find us. Mutiny's a hangin' offense."

"Ever run any cattle?" Tex wanted to know.

"Not since I as a kid. I was born in New Orleans, grew up near San Antone. Rodney tried to tell me all he could."

"I been over the trail to Dodge twice," Tex said, "and to Wyomin' once. I'll be needin' a job."

"You're hired," Rafe said, "if I ever get the money to pay you."

"I'll chance it," Tex Brisco agreed. "I like the way you do things."

"Me for the gold fields in Nevady," Rock said.

"That's good for me," Penn said, "if me and Rock don't strike it rich we may come huntin' a feed."

II

THERE WAS no trail through the tall grass but the one the mind could make, or the instinct of the cattle moving toward water, yet as the long-legged zebra dun moved along the flank of the little herd, Rafe Caradec thought he was coming home.

This was a land for a man to love, a long, beautiful land of rolling grass and trees, of towering mountains, pushing their dark peaks against the sky, and the straight, slim beauty of lodgepole pines.

He sat easy in the saddle, more at home than in many months, for almost half his life had been lived astride a horse, and he liked the dun, which had an easy, space-eating stride. He had won the horse in a poker game in Ogden, and won the saddle and bridle in the same game. The new 1873 Winchester, newest and finest gun on the market, he had bought in San Francisco.

A breeze whispered in the grass, turning it to green and shifting silver as the wind stirred along the bottomland. Rafe heard the gallop of a horse behind him and reined in, turning. Tex Brisco rode up alongside.

"We should be about there, Rafe," he said, digging in his pocket for the makings. "Tell me about that business again, will you?"

Rafe nodded. "Rodney's brand was one he bought from an hombre named Shafter Mason. It was the Bar M. He had two thousand acres in Long Valley that he bought from Red Cloud, paid him good for it, and he

17

was runnin' cattle on that, and some four thousand acres outside the valley. His cabin was built in the entrance to Crazy Woman Canyon.

"He borrowed money, and mortgaged the land, to a man named Bruce Barkow. Barkow's a big cattleman down here, tied in with three or four others. He has several gunmen workin' for him, and Rodney never trusted him, but he was the only man around who could loan him the money he needed."

"What's your plan?" Brisco asked, his eyes following the cattle.

"Tex, I haven't got one. I couldn't plan until I saw the lay of the land. The first thing will be to find Mrs. Rodney and her daughter, and from them, learn what the situation is. Then we can go to work. In the meantime, I aim to sell these cattle and hunt up Red Cloud."

"That'll be tough," Tex suggested. "There's been some Injun trouble, and he's a Sioux. Mostly, they're on the prod right now."

"I can't help it, Tex," Rafe said. "I've got to see him, tell him I have the deed, and explain so's he'll understand. He might turn out to be a good friend, and he would certainly make a bad enemy."

"There may be some question about these cattle," Tex suggested dryly.

"What of it?" Rafe shrugged. "They are all strays, and we culled them out of canyons where no white man has been in years, and slapped our own brand on 'em. We've driven them two hundred miles, so nobody here has any claim on them. Whoever started cattle where we found these left the country a long time ago. You remember what that old trapper told us?"

"Yeah," Tex agreed, "our claim's good enough." He glanced again at the brand, then looked curiously at Rafe. "Man, why didn't you tell me your old man owned the C Bar? When you said to put the C Bar on these cattle you could have knocked me down with an ax! Uncle Joe used to tell me all about the C Bar outfit! The old man had a son who was a ringtailed terror as a kid. Slick with a gun . . . Say!" Tex Brisco stared at Rafe. "You wouldn't be the same one, would you?"

"I'm afraid I am," Rafe said. "For a kid I was too slick with a gun. Had a run-in with some old enemies of Dad's, and when it was over, I hightailed for Mexico."

"Heard about it."

Tex turned his sorrel out in a tight circle to cut a steer back into the herd, and they moved on.

Rafe Caradec rode warily, with an eye on the country. This was all Indian country and the Sioux and Cheyennes had been hunting trouble ever since Custer had ridden into the Black Hills, which was the heart of the Indian country, and almost sacred to the Plains tribes. This was the near end of Long Valley where Rodney's range had begun, and it could be no more than a few miles to Crazy Woman Canyon and his cabin.

Rafe touched a spur to the dun and cantered toward the head of the drive. There were three hundred head of cattle in this bunch, and when the old trapper had told him about them, curiosity had impelled him to have a look. In the green bottom of several adjoining canyons these cattle, remnants of a herd brought into the country several years before, had looked fat and fine.

It had been brutal, bitter work, but he and Tex had rounded up and branded the cattle, then hired two drifting cowhands to help them with the drive.

He passed the man riding point and headed for the strip of trees where Crazy Woman Creek curved out of the canyon and turned in a long sweeping semicircle out to the middle of the valley, then down its center, irrigating some of the finest grass land he had ever seen. Much of it, he noted, was subirrigated from the mountains that lifted on both sides of the valley.

The air was fresh and cool after the long, hot drive over the mountains and desert. The heavy fragrance of the pines and the smell of the long grass shimmering with dew lifted to his nostrils. He moved the dun down to the stream and sat in his saddle while the horse dipped its muzzle into the clear, cold water of the Crazy Woman.

When the gelding lifted his head, Rafe waded him across the stream and climbed the opposite bank, then turned upstream toward the canyon.

The bench beside the stream, backed by its stand of lodgepole pines looked just as Rodney had described it. Yet as the cabin came into sight, Rafe's lips tightened with apprehension, for there was no sign of life. The dun, feeling his anxiety, broke into a canter.

One glance sufficed. The cabin was empty, and evidently had been so for a long time.

Rafe was standing in the door when Tex rode up Brisco glanced around, then at Rafe.

"Well," he said, "looks like we've had a long ride for nothin'."

The other two hands rode up—Johnny Gill and "Bo" Marsh, both Texans. With restless saddles, they had finished a drive in the Wyoming country, then headed west and had ridden clear to Salt Lake. On their return they had run into Rafe and Tex, and hired on to work the herd east to Long Valley.

Gill, a short, leather-faced man of thirty, stared around.

"I know this place," he said. "Used to be the Rodney ranch. Feller name of Dan Shute took over. Rancher."

"Shute, eh?" Tex glanced at Caradec. "Not Barkow?"

Gill shook his head. "Barkow made out to be helpin' Rodney's womenfolks, but he didn't do much good. Personally, I never figgered he cut no great swath a tryin'. Anyway, this here Dan Shute is a bad hombre."

"Well," Rafe said casually, "mebbe we'll find out how bad. I aim to settle right here."

Gill looked at him thoughtfully. "You're buyin' yourself a piece of trouble, mister," he said. "But I never cottoned to Dan Shute, myself. You got any rightful claim to this range? This is where you was headed, ain't it?"

"That's right," Rafe said, "and I have a claim."

"Well, Bo," Gill said, hooking a leg over the saddle-horn, "want to drift on, or do we stay and see how this gent stacks up with Dan Shute?"

Marsh grinned. He had a reckless, infectious grin. "Shore, Johnny," he said. "I'm for stayin' on. Shute's got a big red-headed hand ridin' for him that I never liked, no ways."

"Thanks, boys," Rafe said. "Looks like I've got an out-fit. Keep the cattle in pretty close the next few days. I'm ridin' in to Painted Rock."

"That town belongs to Barkow," Gill advised. "Might pay you to kind of check up on Barkow and Shute. Some of the boys talkin' around the chuckwagon sort of figgered there was more to that than met the eye. That Bruce Barkow is a right important gent around here, but when you read his sign, it don't always add up."

"Mebbe," Rafe suggested, "you'd better come along. Let Tex and Marsh worry with the cattle."

Rafe Caradec turned the dun toward Painted Rock. His liking for the little cattleman Rodney had been very real, and he had come to know and respect the man while aboard the *Mary S.* In the weeks that had followed the flight from the ship, he had been considering the problem of Rodney's ranch so much that it had become much his own problem.

Now, Rodney's worst fears seemed to have been realized. The family had evidently been run off their ranch, and Dan Shute had taken possession. Whether there was any connection between Shute and Barkow remained to be seen, but Caradec knew that chuckwagon gossip can often come close to the truth, and that cowhands often see men more clearly than people who see them only on their good behavior or when in town.

As he rode through the country toward Painted Rock, he studied it curiously, and listened to Johnny Gill's comments. The little Texan had punched cattle in here two seasons, and knew the area better than most.

Painted Rock was the usual cowtown. A double row of weather-beaten, false-fronted buildings, most of which had never been painted, and a few scattered dwellings, some of logs, most of stone. There was a two-story hotel, and a stone building, squat and solid, whose sign identified it as the Painted Rock Bank.

Two buckboards and a spring wagon stood on the street, and a dozen saddle horses stood three-footed at hitching rails. A sign ahead of them and cater-cornered across from the stage station told them that here was the National Saloon.

Gill swung his horse in toward the hitching rail and dropped to the ground. He glanced across his saddle at Caradec.

"The big hombre lookin' us over is the redhead Bo didn't like," he said in a low voice.

Rafe did not look around until he had tied his own horse with a slipknot. Then he hitched his guns into place on his hips. He was wearing two walnut-stocked pistols, purchased in Frisco. He wore jeans, star boots, and a buckskin jacket.

Stepping up on the boardwalk, Rafe glanced at the frank curiosity.

"Howdy, Gill?" he said. "Long time no see."

"Is that bad?" Gill said, and shoved through the doors into the dim, cool interior of the National.

At the bar, Rafe glanced around. Two men stood nearby drinking. Several others were scattered around at tables.

"Red-eye," Gill said, then in a lower tone, "Bruce Barkow is the big man with the black mustache, wearin' black and playin' poker. The Mexican-lookin' hombre across from him is Dan Shute's gun-slingin' segundo, Gee Bonaro."

Rafe nodded, and lifted his glass. Suddenly, he grinned.

"To Charles Rodney!" he said clearly.

Barkow jerked sharply and looked up, his face a shade paler. Bonaro turned his head slowly, like a lizard watching a fly. Gill and Rafe both tossed off their drinks, and ignored the stares.

"Man," Gill said, his eyes dancing, "You don't waste no time, do you?"

Rafe Caradec turned. "By the way, Barkow," he said, "where can I find Mrs. Rodney and her daughter?"

Bruce Barkow put down his cards. "If you've got any business," he said smoothly, "I'll handle it for 'em!"

"Thanks," Rafe said. "My business is personal, and with them."

"Then," Barkow said, his eyes hardening, "you'll have trouble! Mrs. Rodney is dead. Died three months ago."

Rafe's lips tightened. "And her daughter?"

"Ann Rodney," Barkow said carefully, "is here in town. She is to be my wife soon. If you've got any business . . ."

"I'll transact it with her!" Rafe said sharply.

Turning abruptly, he walked out the door, Gill following. The little cowhand grinned, his leathery face folding into wrinkles that belied his thirty-odd years.

"Like I say, Boss," he chuckled, "you shore throw the hooks into 'em!" He nodded toward a building across the street. "Let's try the Emporium. Rodney used to trade there, and Gene Baker who runs it was a friend of his."

The Emporium smelled of leather, dry goods, and all the varied and exciting smells of the general store. Rafe rounded a bale of jeans and walked back to the long counter backed by shelves holding everything from pepper to rifle shells.

"Where can I find Ann Rodney?" he asked.

The white-haired proprietor gave him a quick glance, then nodded to his right. Rafe turned and found him-

23

self looking into the large, soft dark eyes of a slender, yet beautifully shaped girl in a print dress. Her lips were delicately lovely, her dark hair was gathered in a loose knot at the nape of her neck. She was so lovely that it left him a little breathless.

She smiled and her eyes were questioning. "I'm Ann Rodney," she said. "What is it you want?"

"My name is Rafe Caradec," he said gently. "Your father sent me."

Her face went white to the lips and she stepped back suddenly, dropping one hand to the counter as though for support.

"You come—from my *father*? Why, I . . ."

Bruce Barkow, who had apparently followed them from the saloon, stepped in front of Rafe, his face flushed with anger.

"You've scared her to death!" he snapped. "What do you mean, comin' in here with such a story? Charles Rodney has been dead for almost a year!"

Rafe's eyes measured Barkow, his thoughts racing. "He has? How did he die?"

"He was killed," Barkow said, "for the money he was carryin', it looked like." Barkow's eyes turned. "Did you kill him?"

Rafe was suddenly aware that Johnny Gill was staring at him, his brows drawn together, puzzled and wondering. Gill, he realized, knew him but slightly, and might easily become suspicious of his motives.

Gene Baker also was studying him coldly, his eyes alive with suspicion. Ann Rodney stared at him, as if stunned by what he had said, and somehow uncertain.

"No," Rafe said coolly. "I didn't kill him, but I'd be plumb interested to know what made yuh believe he was dead."

"Believe he was dead?" Barkow laughed harshly. "I was with him when he died! We found him beside the trail, shot through the body by bandits. I brought back his belongings to Miss Rodney."

24

"Miss Rodney," Rafe began, "if I could talk to you a few minutes . . ."

"No!" she whispered. "I don't want to talk to you! What can you be thinking of? Coming to me with such a story? What is it you want from me?"

"Somehow," Rafe said quietly, "you've got hold of some false information. Your father has been dead for no more than two months."

"Get out of here!" Barkow ordered, his hands on his gun. "Get out, I say! I don't know what scheme you've cooked up, but it won't work! If you know what's good for you, you'll leave this town while the goin' is good!"

Ann Rodney turned sharply around and ran from the store, heading for the storekeeper's living quarters.

"You'd better get out, mister," Gene Baker said harshly. "We know how Rodney died. You can't work no underhanded schemes on that young lady. Her pa died, and he talked before he died. Three men heard him."

Rafe Caradec turned and walked outside, standing on the boardwalk, frowning at the skyline. He was aware that Gill had moved up beside him.

"Boss," Gill said, "I ain't no lily, but neither am I takin' part in no deal to skin a young lady out of what is hers by rights. You'd better throw a leg over your saddle and get!"

"Don't jump to conclusions, Gill," Rafe advised, "and before you make any change in your plans, suppose you talk to Tex about this? He was with me, an' he knows all about Rodney's death as well as I do. If they brought any belongings off his back here, there's somethin' more to this than we believed."

Gill kicked his boot-toe against a loose board. "Tex was with you? Durn it, man! What of that yarn of theirs? It don't make sense!"

"That's right," Caradec replied, "and before it will we've got to do some diggin'. Johnny," he added, "suppose I told you that Barkow back there held a mortgage on the Rodney ranch, and Rodney went to Frisco, got the money, and paid it in Frisco—then never got home?"

Gill stared at Rafe, his mouth tightening. "Then nobody here would know he ever paid that mortgage but Barkow? The man he paid it to?"

"That's right."

"Then I'd say this Barkow was a sneakin' polecat!" Gill said harshly. "Let's brace him!"

"Not yet, Johnny. Not yet!"

He had anticipated no such trouble, yet if he explained the circumstances of Rodney's death, and was compelled to prove them, he would be arrested for mutiny on the high seas—a hanging offense!

Not only his own life depended on silence, but the lives of Brisco, Penn, and Mullaney.

Yet there must be a way out. There had to be.

III

As Rafe Caradec stood there in the bright sunlight he began to understand a lot of things, and wonder about them. If some of the possessions of Charles Rodney had been returned to Painted Rock, it implied that those who returned them knew something of the shanghaiing of Rodney. How else could they have come by his belongings?

Bully Borger had shanghaied his own crew with the connivance of Hongkong Bohl. Had the man been marked for him? Certainly, it would not be the first time somebody had got rid of a man in such a manner. If that was the true story, it would account for some of Borger's animosity when he had beaten Rodney.

No doubt they had all been part of a plan to make sure that Charles Rodney never returned to San Francisco alive, nor to Painted Rock. Yet believing such a thing and proving it were two vastly different things. Also, it presented a problem of motive. Land was not scarce in the West, and much of it could be had for the taking. Why then, people would ask, would Barkow go to such efforts to get one piece of land?

Rafe had Barkow's signature on the receipt, but that could be claimed to be a forgery. First, a motive beyond the mere value of two thousand acres of land and the money paid on the debt must be established. That might be all, and certainly men had been killed for less, but Bruce Barkow was no fool, nor was he a man who played for small stakes.

Rafe Caradec lighted a cigarette and stared down the street. He must face another fact. Barkow was warned. Whatever he was gambling for, including the girl, was in danger now, and would remain in peril as long as Rafe Caradec remained alive or in the country. That fact stood out cold and clear. Barkow knew by now that he must kill Rafe Caradec.

Rafe understood the situation perfectly. His life had been lived among men who played ruthlessly for the highest stakes. It was no shock to him that men would stoop to killing, or a dozen killings, if they could gain a desired end. From now on he must ride, always aware, and always ready.

Sending Gill to find and buy two pack-horses, Rafe turned on his heel and went into the store. Barkow was gone, and Ann Rodney was still out of sight.

Baker looked up and his eyes held no welcome.

"If you've got any business here," he said, "state it and get out. Charles Rodney was a friend of mine."

"He needed some smarter friends," Rafe replied shortly. "I came here to buy supplies, but if you want to, start askin' yourself some questions. Who profits by Rodney's death? What evidence have you got besides a few of his belongin's that might have been stolen, that he was killed a year ago? How reliable were the three men who were with him? If he went to San Francisco for the money, what were Barkow and the others doin' on the trail?"

"That's neither here nor there," Baker said roughly. "What do you want? I'll refuse no man food."

Coolly, Caradec ordered what he wanted, aware that Baker was studying him. The man seemed puzzled.

"Where you livin'?" Baker asked suddenly. Some of the animosity seemed to have gone from his voice.

"At the Rodney cabin on the Crazy Woman," Caradec said. "I'm stayin', too, till I get the straight of this. If

Ann Rodney is wise she won't get married or get rid of any rights to her property till this is cleared up."

"Shute won't let you stay there."

"I'll stay." Rafe gathered up the box of shells and stowed them in his pocket. "I'll be right there. While you're askin' yourself questions, ask Barkow who holds a mortgage that he claims is unpaid on the Rodney place, lets Dan Shute take over?"

"He didn't want trouble because of Ann," Baker said defensively. "He was right nice about it. He wouldn't foreclose. Givin' her a chance to pay up."

"As long as he's goin' to marry her, why should he foreclose?" Rafe turned away from the counter. "If Ann Rodney wants to see me, I'll tell her all about it, any time. I promised her father I'd take care of her, and I will, whether she likes it or not! Also," he added, "any man who says he talked to Rodney as he was dyin', *lies!*"

The door closed at the front of the store, and Rafe Caradec turned to see the dark, Mexican-looking gunman Gill had indicated in the National Saloon. The man known as Gee Bonaro.

Bonaro came toward him, smiling and showing even white teeth under a thread of mustache.

"Would you repeat that to me, senor?" he asked pleasantly, a thumb hooked in his belt.

"Why not?" Rafe said sharply. He let his eyes, their contempt unveiled, go over the man slowly from head to foot, then back. "If you was one of 'em that said that, you're a liar! And if you touch that gun I'll kill you!"

Gee Bonaro's fingers hovered over the gun butt, and he stood flatfooted, an uncomfortable realization breaking over him. This big stranger was not frightened. In the green eyes was a coldness that turned Bonaro a little sick inside. He was uncomfortably aware that he stood, perilously, on the brink of death.

"Were you one of 'em?" Rafe demanded.

"Si, senor," Bonaro's tongue touched his lips.

"Where was this supposed to be?"

"Where he died, near Pilot Peak, on the trail."

"You're a white-livered liar, Bonaro. Rodney never got back to Pilot Peak. You're bein' trapped for somebody else's gain, and if I were you I'd back up and look the trail over again." Rafe's eyes held the man. "You say you saw him. How was he dressed?"

"Dressed?" Bonaro was confused. Nobody had asked such a thing. He had no idea what to say. Suppose the same question was answered in a different way by one of the others? He wavered and was lost. "I—I don't know. I . . ."

He looked from Baker to Caradec and took a step back, his tongue at his lips, his eyes like those of a trapped animal. The big man facing him somehow robbed him of his sureness, his poise. And he had come here to kill him.

"Rodney talked to me only a few weeks ago, Bonaro," Rafe said coolly. "How many others did he talk to? You're bein' mixed up in a cold-blooded killin', Bonaro! Now turn around and get out! And get out fast!"

Bonaro backed up, and Rafe took a forward step. Wheeling, the man scrambled for the door.

Rafe turned and glanced at Baker. "Think that over," he said coolly. "You'll take the word of a coyote like that about an honest man! Somebody's tryin' to rob Miss Rodney, and because you're believin' that cock and bull story you're helpin' it along."

Gene Baker stood stock-still, his hands still flat on the counter. What he had seen, he would not have believed. Gee Bonaro had slain two men since coming to Painted Rock, and here a stranger had backed him down without lifting a hand or moving toward a gun. Baker rubbed his ear thoughtfully.

Johnny Gill met Rafe in front of the store with two packhorses. A glance told Caradec that the little cowhand had bought well. Gill glanced questioningly at Rafe.

"Did I miss somethin'? I seen that gunhand segundo of Shute's come out of that store like he was chased by the devil. You and him have a run-in?"

"I called him and he backed down," Rafe told Gill. "He said he was one of the three who heard Rodney's last words. I told him he was a liar."

Johnny drew the rope tighter. He glanced out of the corner of his eye at Rafe. This man had come into town and put himself on record for what he was and what he planned faster than anybody he had ever seen.

"Shucks," Johnny said, grinning at the horse, "why go back to Texas? There'll be ruckus enough here, ridin' for that hombre!"

The town of Painted Rock numbered exactly eighty-nine inhabitants, and by sundown the arrival of Rafe Caradec and his challenge to Gee Bonaro was the talk of all of them. It was a behind-the-hand talking, but the story was going the rounds. Also, that Charles Rodney was alive—or had been alive until recently.

By nightfall Dan Shute heard that Caradec had moved into the Rodney house on Crazy Woman, and an hour later he had stormed furiously into his bunkhouse and given Bonaro a tongue-lashing that turned the gunman livid with anger.

Bruce Barkow was worried, and he made no pretense in his conference with Shute. The only hopeful note was that Caradec had said that Rodney was dead.

Gene Baker, sitting in his easy chair in his living quarters behind the store, was uneasy. He was aware that his silence was worrying his wife. He was also aware that Ann was silent herself, an unusual thing, for the girl was usually gay and full of fun and laughter.

The idea that there could have been anything wrong about the story told by Barkow, Weber and Bonaro had never entered the storekeeper's head. He had accepted the story as others had, for many men had been killed along the trails, or had died in fights with Indians. It was another tragedy of the westward march, and he had done what he could—he and his wife had taken Ann Rodney into their home and loved her as their own child.

Now this stranger had come with his questions. Despite Baker's irritation that the matter had come up at all, and despite his outward denials of truth in what Caradec had said, he was aware of an inner doubt that gnawed at the walls of his confidence in Bruce Barkow.

Whatever else he might be, Gene Baker was a fair man. He was forced to admit that Bonaro was not a man in whom reliance could be placed. He was a known gunman, and a suspected outlaw. That Shute hired him was bad enough in itself, yet when he thought of Shute, Baker was again uneasy. The twin ranches of Barkow and Shute surrounded the town on three sides. Their purchases represented no less than fifty per cent of the storekeeper's business, and that did not include what the hands bought on their own.

The drinking of the hands from the ranches supported the National Saloon, too. Gene Baker, who, for all his willingness to live and let live, was a good citizen, or believed he was, found himself examining a situation he did not like. It was not a new situation in Painted Rock, and he had been unconsciously aware of it for some time, yet while aware of it he had tacitly accepted it. Now there seemed to be a larger African in the woodpile, or several of them.

As Baker smoked his pipe, he found himself realizing with some discomfort and growing doubt that Painted Rock was completely subservient to Barkow and Shute. "Pod" Gomer, who was town marshal, had been nominated for the job by Barkow at the council meeting. Joe Benson of the National had seconded the motion, and Dan Shute had calmly suggested that the nomination be closed and Gomer was voted in.

Gene Baker had never liked Gomer but the man was a good gunhand and certainly unafraid. Baker had voted with the others, as had Pat Higley, another responsible citizen of the town.

In the same manner, Benson had been elected mayor of the town, and Roy Gargan had been made judge.

Remembering that the town was actually in the hands of Barkow and Shute, Baker also recalled that at first the tactics of the two big ranchers had caused grumbling among the smaller holders of land. Nothing had ever been done, largely because one of them, Stu Martin, who talked the loudest, had been killed in a fall from a cliff. A few weeks later another small rancher, Al Chase, had mistakenly tried to draw against Bonaro, and had died.

Looked at in that light, the situation made Baker uneasy. Little things began to occur to him that had remained unconsidered, and he began to wonder just what could be done about it even if he knew for sure that Rodney had been killed. Not only was he dependent on Shute and Barkow for business, but Benson, their partner and friend, owned the freight line that brought in his supplies.

Law was still largely a local matter. The Army maintained a fort not too far away, but the soldiers were busy keeping an eye on the Sioux and their allies who were becoming increasingly restive, what with the booming gold camps at Bannack and Alder Gulch, Custer's invasion of the Black Hills, and the steady roll of wagon trains over the Bozeman and Laramie trails.

If there was trouble here, Baker realized with a sudden sickening fear, it would be settled locally. And that meant it would be settled by Dan Shute and Bruce Barkow.

Yet even as he thought of that, Baker recalled the tall man in the black, flat-crowned hat and buckskin jacket.

There was something about Rafe Caradec that was convincing, something that made a man doubt he would be controlled by anybody or anything, at any time, anywhere.

IV

Rafe rode silently alongside Johnny Gill when they moved out of Painted Rock, trailing the two packhorses. The trail turned west by south and crossed the north fork of Clear Creek. They turned then along a narrow path that skirted the huge boulders fringing the mountains.

Gill turned his head slightly. "Might not be a bad idea to take to the hills, Boss," he said carelessly. "There's a trail up thataway—ain't much used, either."

Caradec glanced quickly at the little puncher, then nodded. "All right," he said, "lead off, if you want."

Johnny was riding with his rifle across his saddle, and his eyes were alert. That, Rafe decided, was not a bad idea. He jerked his head back toward Painted Rock.

"What do you think Barkow will do?"

Gill shrugged. "No tellin', but Dan Shute will know what to do. He'll be gunnin' for you if you've sure enough got the straight of this. What you figger happened?"

Rafe hesitated, then he said carefully, "What happened to Charles Rodney wasn't any accident. It was planned and carried out mighty smooth." He waited while the horse took a half dozen steps, then looked up suddenly. "Gill, you size up like a man to ride the river with. Here's the story, and if you ever tell it you'll hang four good men."

Briefly and concisely, he outlined the shanghaiing of

Rodney and himself, the events aboard ship, the escape.

"See?" he added. "It must have looked fool-proof to them. Rodney goes away to sea and never comes back. Nobody but Barkow knows that mortgage was paid, and what did happen was somethin' they couldn't plan for, and probably didn't even think about."

Gill nodded. "Rodney must have been toughern' anybody figgered," he said admiringly. "He never quit tryin', you say?"

"Right. He had only one idea, it looked like, and that was to live to get home to his wife and daughter. If," Rafe added, "the wife was anything like the daughter, I don't blame him!"

The cowhand chuckled. "Yeah, I know what you mean. She's purty as a papoose in a red hat."

"You know, Gill," Rafe said speculatively, "there's one thing that bothers me. Why do they want that ranch so bad?"

"That's got me wonderin', too," Gill agreed. "It's a good ranch, mostly, except for that land at the mouth of the valley. Rises there to a sort of a dome, and the Crazy Woman swings around it. Nothin' much grows there. The rest of it's a good ranch."

"Say anything about Tex or Bo?" Caradec asked.

"No," Gill said. "It figgers like war, now. No use lettin' the enemy know what you're holdin'."

The trail they followed left the grass lands of the creek bottom and turned back up into the hills to a long plateau. They rode on among the tall pines, scattered here and there with birch or aspen along the slopes.

A cool breeze stirred among the pines, and the horses walked slowly, taking their time, their hoof beats soundless on the cushion of pine needles. Once the trail wound down the steep side of a shadowy canyon, weaving back and forth, finally to reach bottom in a brawling, swift-running stream. Willows skirted the banks, and while the horses were drinking, Rafe saw a trout leap in a pool above the rapids. A brown thrasher swept a darting red brown arrow past his head and he could hear yellow warblers gossiping among the willows.

He himself was drinking when he saw the sand crumble from a spot on the bank and fall with a tiny splash into the creek.

Carefully, he got to his feet. His rifle was in his saddle boot, but his pistols were good enough for anything he could see in this narrow place. He glanced casually at Gill, and the cowhand was tightening his cinch, all unaware.

Caradec drew a long breath and hitched up his trousers, then hooked his thumbs in his belt near the gun butts. He had no idea who was there, but that sand did not fall without a reason. In his own mind he was sure that someone was standing in the willow thicket across and downstream, above where the sand had fallen.

Someone was watching them.

"Ready?" Johnny suggested, looking at him curiously.

"Almost," Rafe drawled casually. "Sort of like this little place. It's cool and pleasant. Sort of place a man might like to rest a while, and where a body could watch his back trail, too." He was talking at random, hoping Gill would catch on. The puncher was looking at him intently, now. "At least," Rafe added, "it would be nice here if a man *was* alone. He could think better."

It was then his eye caught the color in the willows. It was a tiny corner of red, a bright, flaming crimson, and it lay where no such color should be.

That was not likely to be a cowhand, unless he was a Mexican or a dude, and they were scarce in this country. It could be an Indian.

If whoever it was had planned to fire, a good chance had been missed while he and Gill drank. Two well-placed shots would have done for them both. Therefore, it was logical to discount the person in the willows as an enemy. Or if so, a patient enemy.

To all appearances whoever lay in the willows preferred to remain unseen. It had all the earmarks of being someone or something trying to avoid trouble.

Gill was quiet and puzzled. Catlike, he watched Rafe for some sign to indicate what the trouble was. A quick scanning of the brush had revealed nothing, but Caradec was not the man to be spooked by a shadow.

"You speak Sioux?" Rafe asked casually.

Gill's mouth tightened. "A mite. Not so good, mebbe."

"Speak loud and say we are friends."

Johnny Gill's eyes were wary as he spoke. There was no sound, no reply.

"Try it again," Rafe suggested. "Tell him we want to talk. Tell him we want to talk to Red Cloud, the great chief."

Gill complied, and there was still no sound. Rafe looked up at him.

"I'm goin' to go over into those willows," he said softly. "Something's wrong."

"You watch yourself!" Gill warned. "The Sioux are plenty smart."

Moving slowly, so as to excite no hostility, Rafe Caradec walked his horse across the stream, then swung down. There was neither sound nor movement from the willows. He walked back among the slender trees, glancing around, yet even then, close as he was, he might not have seen her had it not been for the red stripes. Her clothing blended perfectly with the willows and flowers along the stream bank.

She was a young squaw, slender and dark, with large intelligent eyes. One look told Rafe that she was frightened speechless, and knowing what had happened to squaws found by some of the white men, he could understand.

Her legs were outstretched, and from the marks on the grass and the bank of the stream, he could see she had been dragging herself. The reason was plain to see. One leg was broken just below the knee.

"Johnny," he said, not too loud, "here's a young squaw. She's got a busted leg."

"Better get away quick!" Gill advised. "The Sioux are plenty mean where squaws are concerned."

"Not till I see that leg," Rafe said.

"Boss," Gill advised worriedly, "don't do it. She's liable to yell like blazes if you lay a hand on her. Our lives won't be worth a nickel. We've got troubles enough without askin' for more."

Rafe walked a step nearer, and smiled at the girl. "I want to fix your leg," he said gently, motioning to it. "Don't be afraid."

She said nothing, staring at him, yet he walked up and knelt down. She drew back from his touch and he saw then she had a knife. He smiled and touched the break with gentle fingers.

"Better cut some splints, Gill," he said. "She's got a bad break. Just a little jolt and it might pop right through the skin."

Working carefully, he set the leg. There was no sound from the girl, no sign of pain.

"Nervy, ain't she?" Rafe suggested.

Taking the splints Gill had cut, he bound them on her leg.

"Better take the pack off that paint and split it between the two of us and the other hoss," he said. "We'll put her up on the horse."

When they had her on the paint's back, Gill asked her, in Sioux:

"How far to Indian camp?"

She looked at him, then at Rafe. Then she spoke quickly to him.

Gill grinned. "She says she talks to the chief. That means you. Her camp is about an hour south and west, in the hills."

"Tell her we'll take her most of the way."

Rafe swung into saddle, and they turned their horses back into the trail. Rafe rode ahead, the squaw and the pack-horse following, and Johnny Gill, rifle still across the saddle bows, bringing up the rear.

They had gone no more than a mile when they heard voices, then three riders swung around a bend in the trail, reining in sharply. Tough-looking, bearded men, they stared from Rafe to the Indian girl. She gasped suddenly, and Rafe's eyes narrowed a little.

"See you got our pigeon!" A red-bearded man rode toward them, grinning. "We been chasin' her for a couple of hours. Purty thing, ain't she?"

"Yeah." A slim, wiry man with a hatchet face and a cigarette dangling from his lips was speaking. "Glad you found her. We'll take her off your hands now."

"That's all right," Rafe said quietly. "We're taking her back to her village. She's got a broken leg."

"Takin' her back to the village?" "Red" exclaimed. "Why we cut that squaw out for ourselves and we're slappin' our own brand on her. You get your own squaws." He nodded toward the hatchet faced man. "Get that lead rope, Boyne."

"Keep your hands off that rope!" Rafe's voice was cold. "You blasted fools will get us all killed! This girl's tribe would be down on your ears before night!"

"We'll take care of that!" Red persisted. "Get her, Boyne!"

Rafe smiled suddenly. "If you boys are lookin' for trouble, I reckon you've found it. I don't know how many of you want to die for this squaw, but any time you figger to take her away from us, some of you'd better start sizin' up grave space."

Boyne's eyes narrowed wickedly. "Why, he's askin' for a ruckus, Red! Which eye shall I shoot him through?"

Rafe Caradec sat his horse calmly, smiling a little. "I reckon," he said, "you boys ain't any too battle wise. You're bunched too much. Now, from where I sit, all three of you are dead in range and grouped nice for even one gun shootin', an' I'm figurin' to use two." He spoke to Gill. "Johnny," he said quietly, "suppose these hombres start smokin' it, you take that fat one. Leave the redhead and this Boyne for me."

The fat cowhand shifted in his saddle uncomfortably. He was unpleasantly aware that he had turned his horse so he was sideward to Gill, and while presenting a fair target himself, would have to turn half around in the saddle to fire.

Boyne's eyes were hard and reckless. Rafe knew he was the one to watch. He wore his gun slung low, and that he fancied himself as a gunhand was obvious. Suddenly Rafe knew the man was going to draw.

"Hold it!" A voice cut sharply across the air like the crack of a whip. "Boyne, keep your hand shoulder high! You, too, Red! Now turn your horses and start down the trail. If one of you even looks like you wanted to use a gun, I'll open up with this Henry and cut you into little pieces."

Boyne cursed wickedly. "You're gettin' out of it easy this time!" he said viciously. "I'll see you again!"

Rafe smiled. "Why, sure, Boyne! Only next time you'd better take the rawhide lashin' off the butt of your Colt. Mighty handy when ridin' over rough country, but mighty unhandy when you need your gun in a hurry!"

With a startled gasp, Boyne glanced down. The rawhide thong was tied over his gun to hold it in place. His face two shades whiter than a snake's belly, he turned his horse with his knee and started the trek down the trail.

Bo Marsh stepped out of the brush with his rifle in his hand. He was grinning.

"Hey, Boss! If I'd known that six-gun was tied down, I'd a let you mow him down! That skunk needs it. That's Les Boyne. He's a gunslinger for Dan Shute."

Gill laughed. "Man! Will our ears burn tonight! Rafe's run two of Shute's boys into the ground today!"

Marsh grinned. "Figgered you'd be headed home

soon, and I was out after deer." He glanced at the squaw with the broken leg. "Got more trouble?"

"No," Rafe said. "Those hombres had been runnin' this girl down. She busted her leg gettin' away so we fixed it up. Let's ride."

The trail was smoother now, and drifted casually from one canyon to another. Obviously it had been a game trail which had been found and used by Indians, trappers, and wandering buffalo hunters before the coming of the cowhands and trail drivers.

When they were still several miles from the cabin on the Crazy Woman, the squaw spoke suddenly. Gill looked over at Rafe.

"Her camp's just over that rise in a draw," he said.

Caradec nodded. Then he turned to the girl. She was looking at him, expecting him to speak.

"Tell her," he said, "that we share the land Rodney bought from Red Cloud. That we share it with the daughter of Rodney. Get her to tell Red Cloud we will live on the Crazy Woman, and we are a friend to the Sioux, that their women are safe with us, their horses will not be stolen, that we are a friend to the warriors of Red Cloud and the great chiefs of the Sioux people."

Gill spoke slowly, emphatically, and the girl nodded. Then she turned her horse and rode up through the trees.

"Boss," Johnny said, "she's got our best horse. That's the one I gave the most money for!"

Rafe grinned. "Forget it. The girl was scared silly but wouldn't show it for anything. It's a cheap price to pay to get her home safe. Like I said, the Sioux make better friends than enemies."

When the three men rode up, Tex Brisco was carrying two buckets of water to the house. He grinned at them.

"That grub looks good!" he told them. "I've eaten so much antelope meat the next thing you know I'll be boundin' along over the prairie myself!"

While Marsh got busy with the grub, Johnny told Tex about the events of the trip.

"Nobody been around here," Brisco said. "Yesterday I seen three Injuns, but they was off a couple of miles and didn't come this way. Today there hasn't been nobody around."

During the three days that followed the trip to Painted Rock, Rafe Caradec scouted the range. There were a lot of Bar M cattle around, and most of them were in fairly good shape. His own cattle were mingling freely with them. The range would support many more head than it carried, however, and toward the upper end of Long Valley it was almost untouched. There was much good grass in the mountain meadows, and in several canyons south of the Crazy Woman.

Johnny Gill and Bo Marsh explained the lay of the land as they knew it.

"North of here," Gill said, "back of Painted Rock, and mostly west of there, the mountains rise up nigh onto nine thousand feet. Good huntin' country, some of the best I ever seen. South, toward the end of the valley, the mountains thin out. There's a pass through to the head of Otter Creek and that country west of the mountains is good grazin' land, and nobody much in there yet. Injuns got a big powwow grounds over there.

"Still further south, there's a long red wall, runnin' purty much north and south. Only one entrance in thirty-five miles. Regular hole in the wall. A few men could get into that hole and stand off an army, and if they wanted to hightail it, they could lose themselves in back country."

Rafe scouted the crossing toward the head of Otter Creek and rode down the creek to the grass lands below. This would be good grazing land, and mentally he made a note to make some plans for it.

He rode back to the ranch that night and when he was sitting on the stoop after the sun was down, he

43

looked around at Tex Brisco. "You been over the trail from Texas?" he asked.

"Uh-huh."

"Once aboard ship you was tellin' me about a stampede you had. Only got back about sixteen hundred head of a two-thousand-head herd. That sort of thing happen often?"

Tex laughed. "Shucks, yes! Stampedes are regular things along the trail. You lose some cattle, you mebbe get more back, but there's plenty of maverick stock runnin' on the plains south of the Platte—all the way to the Canadian, as far as that goes."

"Reckon a few men could slip over there and round up some of that stock?"

Brisco sat up and glanced at Rafe. "Shore could. Wild stuff, though, and it would be a man-sized job."

"Mebbe," Caradec suggested, "we'll try and do it. It would be one way of gettin' a herd pretty fast, or turnin' some quick money."

V

THERE WERE days of hard, driving labor. Always, one man stayed at the cabin keeping a sharp lookout for any of the Shute or Barkow riders. Caradec knew they would come, and when they did come they would be riding with only one idea in mind—to get rid of him.

In that visit to Painted Rock he had laid his cards on the table, and they had no idea how much he knew, or what his story of Charles Rodney could be. Rafe Caradec knew Barkow was worried, and that pleased him. Yet while the delayed attack was a worry, it was also a help.

There was some grumbling from the hands, but he kept them busy cutting hay in the meadows, and stacking it. Winter in this country was going to be bad—he needed no weather prophet to tell him that—and he had no intention of losing a lot of stock.

In a canyon that branched off from the head of Crazy Woman, he had found a warm spring. There was small chance of it freezing, yet the water was not too hot to drink. In severe cold it would freeze, but otherwise it would offer an excellent watering place for his stock. They made no effort to bring hay back to the ranch, but stacked it in huge stacks back in the canyons and meadows.

There had been no sign of Indians. It seemed as if they had moved out and left the country.

Then one night he heard a noise at the corral, and the snorting of a horse. Instantly he was out of bed and

45

had his boots on when he heard Brisco swearing in the next room. They got outside in a hurry, fearing someone was rustling their stock. In the corral they could see the horses, and there was no one nearby.

Bo Marsh had walked over to the corral, and suddenly he called out.

"Boss! Lookit here!"

They all trooped over, then stopped. Instead of five horses in the corral there were ten!

One of them was the paint they had loaned the young squaw, but the others were strange horses, and every one a picked animal.

"Well, I'll be durned!" Gill exploded. "Brung back our own horse and an extry one for each of us. Reckon that big black is for you, Boss."

By daylight when they could examine the horses, Tex Brisco walked around them admiringly.

"Man," he said, "that was the best horse trade I ever heard of! There's four of the purtiest horses I ever laid an eye on! I always did say the Sioux knowed horse flesh, and this proves it."

Rafe studied the valley thoughtfully. They would have another month of good haying weather if there was no rain. Four men could not work much harder than they were, but the beaver were building their houses bigger and in deeper water, and from that and all other indications the winter was going to be hard.

He made his decision suddenly. "I'm ridin' to Painted Rock. Want to come along, Tex?"

"Yeah." The Texan looked at him calculatingly. "Yeah, I'd like that."

"How about me?" Bo asked, grinning. "Johnny went last time. I could shore use a belt of that red-eye the National peddles, and mebbe a look around town."

"Take him along, Boss," Johnny said. "I can hold this end. If he stays he'll be ridin' me all the time, anyway."

"All right. Saddle up first thing in the mornin'."

"Boss—" Johnny threw one leg over the other and

lighted his smoke. "One thing I better tell you. I hadn't said a word before but two, three days ago when I was down to the bend of the Crazy Woman I run into a couple of fellers. One of 'em was Red Blazer, that big galoot who was with Boyne. Remember?"

Rafe turned around and looked down at the little leather-faced cowhand.

"Well," he said, "what about him?"

Gill took a long drag on his cigarette. "He told me he was carryin' a message from Trigger Boyne, and that Trigger was goin' to shoot on sight, next time you showed up in Painted Rock."

Rafe reached over on the table and picked up a piece of cold cornbread.

"Then I reckon that's what he'll do," he said. "If he gets into action fast enough."

"Boss," Marsh pleaded, "if that red-headed Tom Blazer, brother to the one you had the run in with—if he's there, I want him."

"That the one we saw on the National stoop?" Rafe asked Gill.

"Uh-huh. There's five of them brothers. All gun-toters."

Gill got up and stretched. "Well, I'll have it purty lazy while you hombres are down there dustin' lead." He added, "It would be a good idea to sort of keep an eye out. Gee Bonaro's still in town and feelin' mighty mad."

Rafe walked outside, strolling toward the corral. Behind him, Marsh turned to Gill.

"Reckon he can sling a gun?"

Tex chuckled. "Mister, that hombre killed one of the fastest, slickest gun throwers that ever came out of Texas, and done it when he was no more'n sixteen, down on the C Bar. And also, while I've never seen him shoot, if he can shoot like he can fist-fight, Mr. Trigger Boyne had better grab hisself an armful of hossflesh and start makin' tracks for the blackest part of the Black Hills—*fast!*"

Nothing about the town of Painted Rock suggested drama or excitement. It lay sprawled comfortably in the morning sunlight in an elbow of Rock Creek. A normally roaring and plunging stream, the creek had decided here to loiter a while, enjoying the warm sun and the graceful willows that lined the banks.

Behind and among the willows the white slender trunks of the birch trees marched in neat ranks, each tree so like its neighbor that it was almost impossible to distinguish between them. Clumps of mountain alder, yellow rose, puffed clematis and antelope bush were scattered along the far bank of the stream, and advanced up the hill beyond in skirmishing formation.

In a few weeks now the aspen leaves would be changing, and Painted Rock would take on a background of flaming color—a bank of trees, rising toward the darker growth of spruce and fir along the higher mountainside.

Painted Rock's one street was the only thing about the town that was ordered. It lay between two neat rows of buildings which stared at each other down across a long lane of dust and during the rainy periods, of mud.

At any time of day or night a dozen saddle horses would be standing three-legged at the hitching rails, usually in front of Joe Benson's National Saloon. A buckboard or a spring wagon would also be present, usually driven by some small rancher in for his supplies. The two big outfits sent two wagons together, drawn by mules.

Bruce Barkow sat in front of the sheriff's office this morning, deep in conversation with Pod Gomer. It was a conversation that had begun over an hour before.

Gomer was a short, thick-set man, almost as deep from chest to spine as from shoulder to shoulder. He was not fat, and was considered a tough man to tangle with. He was also a man who liked to play on the winning side, and long ago he had decided there was only one side to consider in this fight—the side of Dan Shute and Bruce Barkow.

Yet he was a man who was sensitive to the way the wind blew, and he frequently found himself puzzled when he considered his two bosses. There was no good feeling between them. They met on business or pleasure, saw things through much the same eyes, but each wanted to be king pin. Sooner or later, Gomer knew, he must make a choice between them.

Barkow was shrewd, cunning. He was a planner and a conniver. He was a man who would use any method to win, but in most cases he kept himself in the background of anything smacking of crime or wrongdoing. Otherwise, he was much in the foreground.

Dan Shute was another type of man. He was tall and broad of shoulder. Normally he was sullen, hard-eyed, and surly. He had little to say to anyone, and was more inclined to settle matters with a blow or a gun than with words. He was utterly cold-blooded, felt slightly about anything, and would kill a man as quickly and with as little excitement as he would brand a calf.

Barkow might carve a notch on his gun butt. Shute wouldn't even understand such a thing.

Shute was a man who seemed to be without vanity, and such men are dangerous. For the vanity is there, only submerged, and the slow-burning, deep fire of hatred for the vain smolder within them until suddenly they burst into flame and end in sudden, dramatic and ugly climax and violence.

Pod Gomer understood little of Dan Shute. He understood the man's complete character just enough to know that he was dangerous, that as long as Shute rode along, Barkow would be top dog, but that if ever Barkow incurred Shute's resentment, the deep-seated fury of the gunman would brush his partner aside as he would swat a fly. In a sense, both men were using each other, but of the two, Dan Shute was the man to be reckoned with.

Yet Gomer had seen Barkow at work. He had seen how deviously the big rancher planned, how carefully he made friends. At the Fort, they knew and liked him, and what little law there was outside the town of Painted Rock was in the hands of the commanding officer at the fort. Knowing this, Bruce Barkow had made it a point to know the personnel there, and to plan accordingly.

The big black which Rafe was riding was a powerful horse, and he let the animal have its head. Behind him in single file, trailed Tex Brisco and Bo Marsh.

Rafe Caradec was thinking as he rode. He had seen too much of violence and struggle to fail to understand men who lived life along the frontier. He had correctly gauged the kind of courage Gee Bonaro possessed, yet he knew the man was dangerous, and if the opportunity offered would shoot and shoot instantly.

"Trigger" Boyne was another proposition. Boyne was reckless, wickedly fast with a gun, and the type of man who would fight at the drop of a hat, and had his own ready to drop on the slightest pretext. Boyne liked the name of being a gunman, and he liked being top dog. If Boyne had sent a warning to Caradec it would be only because he intended to back up that warning.

Rafe took the black along the mountain trail, riding swiftly. The big horse was the finest he had ever had between his knees. When a Sioux gave gifts, he apparently went all the way. A gift had been sent to each of the men on the Crazy Woman, which was evidence that the Sioux had looked them over at home.

The black had a long, space-eating stride that seemed to put no strain on his endurance. The horses given to the others were almost as good. There were not four men in the mountains mounted as well, Rafe knew.

He rounded the big horse into the dusty street of

Painted Rock and rode down toward the hitching rail at a spanking trot. He pulled up and swung down, and the other men swung down alongside him.

"Just keep your eyes open," Rafe said guardedly. "I don't want trouble. But if Boyne starts anything, he's my meat."

Marsh nodded and walked up on the boardwalk alongside of Brisco, who was sweeping the street with quick, observant eyes.

"Have a drink?" Rafe suggested, and led the way inside the National.

Joe Benson was behind the bar. He looked up warily as the three men entered. He spoke to Bo; then glanced at Tex Brisco. He placed Tex as a stranger, and his mind leaped ahead. It took no long study to see that Tex was a hard character, and a fighting man.

Joe was cautious and shrewd. Unless he was mistaken, Barkow and Shute had their work cut out for them. These men didn't look like the sort to back water for anything or anyone. The town's saloonkeeper-mayor had an uncomfortable feeling that a change was in the offing, yet he pushed the feeling aside with irritation.

That must not happen. His own future and his own interests were too closely allied to those of Barkow and Shute.

Of course, when Barkow married the Rodney girl that would give them complete title to the ranch. That would leave them in the clear and these men, if alive, could be run off the ranch with every claim to legal process.

Caradec tossed off his whisky and looked up sharply. His glance pinned Joe Benson to the spot.

"Trigger Boyne sent word he was looking for me," he said abruptly. "Tell him I'm in town—ready!"

"How should I know Trigger better'n any other man who comes into this bar?" Benson demanded.

"You know him. Tell him."

Rafe hitched his guns into a comfortable position and

strode through the swinging doors. There were a dozen men in sight but none of them resembled Boyne or either of the Blazers he had seen.

He started for the Emporium. Behind him Tex stopped by one of the posts that supported the wooden awning over the walk, and leaned a negligent shoulder against it, a cigarette drooping from the corner of his mouth.

Bo Marsh sat back in a chair against the wall, his interested eyes sweeping the street. Several men, who passed spoke to him and glanced at Tex Brisco's tall, lean figure.

Rafe opened the door of the Emporium and strode inside. Gene Baker looked up, frowning when he saw him. He was not glad to see Rafe, for the man's words on his previous visit had been responsible for some doubts and speculations.

"Is Ann Rodney in?"

Baker hesitated. "Yes," he said finally. "She's back there."

Rafe went around the counter toward the door, hat in his left hand.

"I don't think she wants to see you," Baker advised.

"All right," Rafe said, "we'll see."

He pushed past the screen and stepped into the living room beyond.

Ann Rodney was sewing, and when the quick step sounded, she glanced up. Her eyes changed. Something inside her seemed to turn over slowly. This big man who had brought such disturbing news affected her as no man ever had. Considering her engagement to Bruce Barkow, she didn't like to feel that way about any man. Since he had last been here she had worried a good deal about what he had said and her reaction to it. Why would he come with such a tale? Shouldn't she have heard him out?

Bruce said that the man was an impostor and someone who hoped to get money from her. Yet she knew something of Johnny Gill and she had danced with Bo Marsh, and knew that these men were honest. They had been liked and respected in Painted Rock.

"Oh," she said, rising. "It's you?"

Rafe stopped in the center of the room, a tall picturesque figure in his buckskin coat and with his waving black hair. He was, she thought, a handsome man. He wore his guns low and tied down, and she knew what that meant.

"I was goin' to wait," he said abruptly, "and let you come to me and ask questions, if you ever did, but when I thought it over, rememberin' what I'd promised your father, I decided I must come back now, lay all my cards on the table, and tell you what happened."

She started to speak, and he lifted his hand. "Wait. I'm goin' to talk quick, because in a few minutes I have an appointment outside that I must keep. Your father did not die on the trail back from California. He was shanghaied in San Francisco, taken aboard a ship while unconscious and forced to work as a seaman. I was shanghaied at the same time and place. Your father and I in the months that followed were together a lot. He asked me to come here, to take care of you and his wife, and to protect you. He died of beatin's he got aboard ship, just before the rest of us got away from the ship. I was with him when he died, settin' beside his bed. Almost his last words were about you."

Ann Rodney stood very still, staring at him. There was a ring of truth in the rapidly spoken words, yet how could she believe this? Three men had told her they saw her father die, and one of them was the man she was to marry, the man who had befriended her, who had refused to foreclose on the mortgage he held and take from her the last thing she possessed in the world.

"What was my father like?" she asked.

"Like?" Rafe's brow furrowed. "How can anybody weigh what any man is like. I'd say he was about five feet eight or nine. When he died his hair was almost white, but when I first saw him he had only a few gray hairs. His face was a heap like yours. So were his eyes, except they weren't so large nor so beautiful. He was a kind man who wasn't used to violence and he didn't like it. He planned well, and thought well, but the West was not the country for him, yet. Ten years from now when it has settled more, he'd have been a leadin' citizen. He was a good man, and a sincere man."

"It sounds like him," Ann said hesitantly, "but there is nothing you could not have learned here, or from someone who knew him."

"No," he said frankly. "That's so. But there's somethin' else you should know. The mortgage your father had against his place was paid."

"What?" Ann stiffened. "Paid? How can you say that?"

"He borrowed the money in Frisco and paid Barkow with it. He got a receipt for it."

"Oh, I can't believe that! Why, Bruce would have . . ."

"Would he?" Rafe asked gently. "You sure?"

She looked at him. "What was the other thing?"

"I have a deed," he said, "to the ranch, made out to you and to me."

Her eyes widened, then hardened with suspicion. "So? Now things become clearer. A deed to my father's ranch made out to you and to me! In other words, you are laying claim to half of my ranch?"

"Please . . ." Rafe said. "I . . ."

She smiled. "You needn't say anything more, Mr. Caradec. I admit I was almost coming to believe there was something in your story. At least, I was wondering about it, for I couldn't understand how you hoped to profit from any such tale. Now it becomes clear. You are trying to get half my ranch. You have even moved into my house without asking permission."

She stepped to one side of the door.

"I'm sorry, but I must ask you to leave! I must also ask you to vacate the house on Crazy Woman at once!

I must ask you to refrain from calling on me again, or from approaching me."

"You're jumping to conclusions. I never aimed to claim any part of the ranch! I came here only because your father asked me to."

"Good day, Mr. Caradec!" Ann still held the curtain.

He looked at her, and for an instant their eyes held. She was first to look away. He turned abruptly and stepped through the curtain, and as he did the door opened and he saw Bo Marsh.

Marsh's eyes were excited and anxious. "Rafe," he said, "that Boyne hombre's in front of the National. He wants you!"

"Why shore," Rafe said quietly. "I'm ready."

He walked to the front door, hitching his guns into place. Behind him, he heard Ann Rodney asking Baker:

"What did he mean? That Boyne was waiting for him?"

Baker's reply came to Rafe as he stepped out into the morning light.

"Trigger Boyne's goin' to kill him, Ann. You'd better go back inside!"

Rafe smiled slightly. Kill him? Would that be it? No man knew better than he the tricks that Destiny plays on a man, or how often the right man dies at the wrong time and place. A man never wore a gun without inviting trouble, he never stepped into a street and began the gunman's walk without the full knowledge that he might be a shade too slow, that some small thing might disturb him just long enough!

VI

MORNING SUN was bright and the street lay empty of horses or vehicles. A few idlers loafed in front of the stage station, but all of them were on their feet.

Rafe Caradec saw his black horse switch his tail at a fly, and he stepped down in the street. Trigger Boyne stepped off the boardwalk to face him, some distance off. Rafe did not walk slowly, he made no measured, quiet approach. He started to walk toward Boyne, going fast.

Trigger stepped down into the street easily, casually. He was smiling. Inside, his heart was throbbing and there was a wild reckless eagerness within him. This one he would finish off fast. This would be simple, easy.

He squared in the street, and suddenly the smile was wiped from his face. Caradec was coming toward him, shortening the distance at a fast walk. That rapid approach did something to the calm on Boyne's face and in his mind. It was wrong. Caradec should have come slowly, he should have come poised and ready to draw.

Knowing his own deadly marksmanship, Boyne felt sure he could kill this man at any distance. But as soon as he saw that walk, he knew that Caradec was going to be so close in a few more steps that he himself would be killed.

It is one thing to know you are to kill another man,

quite a different thing to know you are to die yourself. If Caradec walked that way he would be so close he couldn't miss!

Boyne's legs spread and the wolf sprang into his eyes, but there was panic there, too. He had to stop his man, get him now. His hand swept down for his gun.

Yet something was wrong. For all his speed he seemed incredibly slow, because that other man, that tall, moving figure in the buckskin coat and black hat, was already shooting.

Trigger's own hand moved first, his own hand gripped the gun butt first, and then he was staring into a smashing, blossoming rose of flame that seemed to bloom beyond the muzzle of that big black gun in the hands of Rafe Caradec. Something stabbed at his stomach, and he went numb to his toes.

Stupidly he swung his gun up, staring over it. The gun seemed awfully heavy. He must get a smaller one. That gun opposite him blossomed with rose again and something struck him again in the stomach. He started to speak, half turning toward the men in front of the stage station, his mouth opening and closing.

Something was wrong with him, he tried to say. Why, everyone knew he was the fastest man in Wyoming, unless it was Shute! Everyone knew that! The heavy gun in his hand bucked and he saw the flame stab at the ground. He dropped the gun, swayed, then fell flat on his face.

He would have to get up. He was going to kill that stranger, that Rafe Caradec. He would have to get up.

The numbness from his stomach climbed higher and he suddenly felt himself in the saddle of a bucking horse, a monstrous and awful horse that leaped and plunged and it was going up! Up! Up!

Then it came down hard, and he felt himself leave the saddle, all sprawled out. The horse had thrown him. Bucked off into the dust. He closed his hands spasmodically.

Rafe Caradec stood tall in the middle of the gunman's walk, the black, walnut-stocked pistol in his right hand. He glanced once at the still figure sprawled in the street, then his eyes lifted, sweeping the walks in swift, accurate appraisal. Only then, some instinct prodded his subconscious and warned him. The merest flicker of a curtain, and in the space between the curtain and the edge of the window, the black muzzle of a rifle!

His .44 lifted and the heavy gun bucked in his hand just as flame leaped from the rifle barrel and he felt quick urgent fingers pluck at his sleeve. The .44 jolted again, and a rifle rattled on the shingled porch roof. The curtain made a tearing sound, and the head and shoulders of a man fell through, toppling over the sill. Overbalanced, the heels came up and the man's body rolled over slowly, seemed to hesitate, then rolled over again, poised an instant on the edge of the roof and dropped suddenly into the dust.

Dust lifted from around the body, settled back. Gee Bonaro thrust hard with one leg, and his face twisted a little.

In the quiet street there was no sound, no movement. For the space of a full half-minute, the watchers held themselves, shocked by the sudden climax, stunned with unbelief. Gee Bonaro had made his try, and died.

Rafe Caradec turned slowly and walked back to his horse. Without a word he swung into saddle. He turned the horse and, sitting tall in the saddle, swept the street with a cold, hard eye that seemed to stare at each man there. Then, as if by his own wish, the black horse turned. Walking slowly, his head held proudly, he carried his rider down the street and out of town.

Behind him, coolly and without smiles, Bo Marsh and Tex Brisco followed. Like him, they rode slowly, like him they rode proudly. Something in their bearing seemed to say, "We were challenged, we came. You see the result."

In the window of the National, Joe Benson chewed

58

his mustache. He stared at the figure of Trigger Boyne with vague disquiet, then irritation.

"Damn it!" he muttered under his breath. "You was supposed to be a gunman? What in thunder was wrong with you?"

A bullet from Boyne's gun, or from Bonaro's for that matter, could have ended it all. A bullet now could settle the whole thing, quiet the gossip, remove the doubts, and leave Barkow free to marry Ann, and the whole business could go forward. Instead, they had failed.

It would be a long time now, Benson knew, before it was all over. A long time. Barkow was slipping. The man had better think fast and get something done. Rafe Caradec must die.

The Fort Laramie Treaty of 1868 had forbidden white men to enter the Powder River country, yet gold discoveries brought prospectors north in increasing numbers. Small villages and mining camps had come into existence. Following them, cattlemen discovered the rich grasses of northern Wyoming and a few herds came over what later was to be known as the Texas Trail.

Indian attacks and general hostility caused many of these pioneers to retreat to more stable localities, but a few of the more courageous had stayed on. Prospectors had entered the Black Hills following the Custer expedition in 1874, and the Sioux always resentful of any incursion upon their hunting grounds or any flaunting of their rights, were preparing to do something more than talk.

The names of such chiefs as Red Cloud, Dull Knife, Crazy Horse and the medicine man, Sitting Bull, came more and more into frontier gossip. A steamboat was reported to be en route up the turbulent Yellowstone and river traffic on the upper Missouri was an accepted fact. There were increasing reports of gatherings of Indians in the hills, and white men rode warily, never without arms.

Cut off from contact with the few scattered ranchers, Rafe Caradec and his riders heard little of the gossip except what they gleaned from an occasional prospector or wandering hunter. Yet no gossip was needed to tell them how the land lay.

Twice they heard sounds of rifle fire, and once the Sioux ran off a number of cattle from Shute's ranch, taking them from a herd kept not far from Long Valley. Two of Shute's riders were killed. None of Caradec's cattle were molested. He was left strictly alone. Indians avoided his place, no matter what their mission.

Twice, riders from the ranch went to Painted Rock. Each time they returned they brought stories of an impending Indian outbreak. A few of the less courageous ranchers sold out and left the country. In all this time, Rafe Caradec lived in the saddle, riding often from dawn until dusk, avoiding the tangled brakes, but studying the lay of the land with care.

There was, he knew, some particular reason for Bruce Barkow's interest in the ranch that belonged to Ann Rodney. What the reason was, he must know. Without it, he knew he could offer no real reason why Barkow would go to the lengths he had gone to get a ranch that was, on the face of things, of no more value than any piece of land in the country, most of which could be had for the taking. . . .

Ann spent much of her time alone. Business at the store was thriving and Gene Baker and his wife, and often Ann as well, were busy. In her spare time the thought kept returning to her that Rafe Caradec might be honest.

Yet she dismissed the thought as unworthy. If she admitted even for an instant that he was honest, she must also admit that Bruce Barkow was dishonest. A thief, and possibly a killer. Yet somehow the picture of her father kept returning to her mind. It was present there on one of the occasions when Bruce Barkow came to call.

A handsome man, Barkow understood how to appeal to a woman. He carried himself well, and his clothes were always the best in Painted Rock. He called this evening looking even better than he had on the last occasion, his black suit neatly pressed, his mustache carefully trimmed.

They had been talking for some time when Ann mentioned Rafe Caradec.

"His story sounded so sincere!" she said, after a minute. "He said he had been shanghaied in San Francisco with Father, and that they had become acquainted on the ship."

"He's a careful man," Barkow commented, "and a dangerous one. He showed that when he killed Trigger Boyne and Bonaro. He met Boyne out on the range, and they had some trouble over an Indian girl."

"An Indian girl?" Ann looked at him questioningly.

"Yes," Barkow frowned as if the subject was distasteful to him. "You know how some of the cowhands are—always running after some squaw. They have stolen squaws, kept them for a while, then turned them loose or killed them. Caradec had a young squaw and Boyne tried to argue with him to let her go. They had words, and there'd have been a shooting then if one of Caradec's other men hadn't come up with a rifle, and Shute's boys went away."

Ann was shocked. She had heard of such things happening, and was well aware of how much trouble they caused. That Rafe Caradec would be a man like that was hard to believe. Yet, what did she know of the man?

He disturbed her more than she allowed herself to believe. Despite the fact that he seemed to be trying to work some scheme to get all or part of her ranch, and despite all she had heard of him at one time or another from Bruce, she couldn't make herself believe that all she heard was true.

That he appealed to her, she refused to admit. Yet when with him, she felt drawn to him. She liked his rugged masculinity, his looks, his voice, and was impressed with his sincerity. Yet the killing of Boyne and Bonaro was the talk of the town.

The Bonaro phase of the incident she could understand from the previous episode in the store. But no one had any idea of why Boyne should be looking for Caradec. The solution now offered by Barkow was the only one. A fight over a squaw! Without understanding why, Ann felt vaguely resentful.

For days a dozen of Shute's riders hung around town. There was talk of lynching Caradec, but nothing came of it. Ann heard the talk, and asked Baker about it.

The old storekeeper looked up, nodding.

"There's talk, but it'll come to nothin'. None of these boys aim to ride out there to Crazy Woman and tackle that crowd. You know what Gill and Marsh are like. They'll fight, and they can. Well, Caradec showed what he could do with a gun when he killed those two in the street. I don't know whether you saw that other feller with Caradec or not. The one from Texas. Well, if he ain't tougher than either Marsh or Gill, I'll pay off! Notice how he wore his guns? Nope, nobody'll go looking for them. If they got their hands on Caradec that would be somethin' else."

Baker rubbed his jaw thoughtfully. "Unless they are powerful lucky, they won't last long, anyway. That's Injun country, and Red Cloud or Man Afraid of His Hoss won't take kindly to white men livin' there. They liked your pa, and he was friendly to 'em."

As a result of his conversations with Barkow, Sheriff Pod Gomer had sent messages south by stage to Cheyenne and the telegraph. Rafe Caradec had come from San Francisco, and Bruce Barkow wanted to know who and what he was. More than that, he wanted to find out how he had been allowed to escape the *Mary S.* With that in mind he wrote to Bully Borger.

Borger had agreed to take Charles Rodney to sea and let him die there, silencing the truth forever. Allowing Rafe Caradec to come ashore with his story was not keeping the terms of his bargain. If Caradec had actually been aboard the ship, and left it, there might be something in that to make him liable to the law.

Barkow intended to leave no stone unturned. And in the meantime, he spread his stories around about Caradec's reason for killing Boyne.

Caradec went on with his haying. The nights were already growing more chill. At odd times when not haying or handling cattle, he and the boys built another room to the cabin, and banked the house against the wind. Fortunately, its position was sheltered. Wind would not bother them greatly where they were, but there would be snow and lots of it.

Rafe rode out each day, and several times brought back deer or elk. The meat was jerked and stored away. Gill got the old wagon Rodney had brought from Missouri and made some repairs. It would be the easiest way to get supplies out from Painted Rock. He worked over it, and soon had it in excellent shape.

On the last morning of the month, Rafe walked out to where Gill was hitching a team to the wagon.

"Looks good," he agreed. "You've done a job on it, Johnny."

Gill looked pleased. He nodded at the hubs of the wheels. "Notice 'em? No squeak!"

"Well, I'll be hanged!" Rafe looked at the grease on the hubs. "Where'd you get the grease?"

"Sort of a spring back over in the hills. I brung back a bucket of it."

Rafe Caradec looked up sharply. "Johnny, where'd yuh find that spring?"

"Why"—Gill looked puzzled—"it's just a sort of hole

like, back over next to that mound. You know, in that bad range. Ain't much account down there, but I was down there once and found this here spring. This stuff works as well as the grease you buy."

"It should," Rafe said dryly. "It's the same stuff!"

He caught up the black and threw a saddle on it. Within an hour he was riding down toward the barren knoll Gill had mentioned. What he found was not a spring, but a hole among some sparse rushes, dead and sick-looking. It was an oil seepage.

Oil!

This then, could be the reason why Barkow and Shute were so anxious to acquire title to this piece of land, so anxious that they would have a man shanghaied and killed. Caradec recalled that Bonneville had reported oil seepage on his trip through the state some forty years or so before, and there had been a well drilled in the previous decade.

One of the largest markets for oil was the patent medicine business, for it was the main ingredient in so-called "British Oil."

The hole in which the oil was seeping in a thick stream might be shallow, but sounding with a six-foot stick found no bottom. Rafe doubted if it was much deeper. Still, there would be several barrels here, and he seemed to recall some talk of selling oil for twenty dollars the barrel.

Swinging into the saddle, he turned the big black down the draw and rode rapidly toward the hills. This could be the reason, for certainly it was reason enough. The medicine business was only one possible market, for machinery of all kinds needed lubricants. There was every chance that the oil industry might really mean something in time.

If the hole was emptied, how fast would it refill? And how constant was the supply? On one point he could soon find out.

He swung the horse up out of the draw, forded the

Crazy Woman, and cantered up the hill to the cabin. As he reined in and swung down at the door he noticed two strange horses.

Tex Brisco stepped to the door, his face hard.

"Watch it, Boss!" he said sharply.

Pod Gomer's thick-set body thrust into the doorway. "Caradec," he said calmly, "you're under arrest."

Rafe swung down, facing him. Two horses. Who had ridden the other one?

"For what?" he demanded.

His mind was racing. The mutiny? Had they found out about that?

"For killin'. Shootin' Bonaro."

"*Bonaro?*" Rafe laughed. "You mean for defendin' myself? Bonaro had a rifle in that window. He was all set to shoot me!"

Gomer nodded coolly. "That was most folks' opinion, but it seems nobody *saw* him aim any gun at you. We've only got your say-so. When we got to askin' around, it begun to look sort of funny like. It appears to a lot of folks that you just took that chance to shoot him and get away with it. Anyway, you'd be better off to stand trial."

"Don't go, Boss," Brisco said. "They don't ever aim to have a trial."

"You'd better not resist," Gomer replied calmly. "I've got twenty Shute riders down the valley. I made 'em stay back. The minute any shootin' starts, they'll come a runnin', and you all know what that would mean."

Rafe knew. It would mean the death of all four of them and the end to any opposition to Barkow's plans. Probably that was what the rancher hoped would happen.

"Why, sure, Gomer," Caradec said calmly. "I'll go."

Tex started to protest, and Rafe saw Gill hurl his hat into the dust.

"Give me your guns then," Gomer said, "and mount up."

"No." Rafe's voice was flat. "I keep my guns till I get to town. If that bunch of Shute's starts anything, the first one I'll kill will be you, Gomer!"

Pod Gomer's face turned sullen. "You ain't goin' to be bothered. I'm the law here. Let's go!"

"Gomer," Tex Brisco said viciously, "if anything happens to him, I'll kill you and Barkow both!"

"That goes for me, too!" Gill said harshly.

"And me!" Marsh put in. "I'll get you if I have to drygulch you, Gomer."

"Well, all right!" Gomer said angrily. "It's just a trial. I told 'em I didn't think much of it, but the judge issued the warrant."

He was scowling blackly. It was all right for them to issue warrants, but if they thought he was going to get killed for them, they were bloody well wrong!

Pod Gomer jammed his hat down on his head. This was a far cry from the coal mines of Lancashire, but sometimes he wished he was back in England. There was a look in Brisco's eyes he didn't like.

"No," he told himself, "he'll be turned loose before I take a chance. Let Barkow kill his own pigeons. I don't want these Bar M hands gunnin' for *me!*"

The man who had ridden the other horse stepped out of the cabin, followed closely by Bo Marsh. There was no smile on the young cowhand's face. The man was Bruce Barkow.

For an instant, his eyes met Caradec's. "This is just a formality," Barkow said smoothly. "There's been some talk around Painted Rock and a trial will clear the air a lot, and of course if you're innocent, Caradec, you'll be freed."

"You sure of that?" Rafe's eyes smiled cynically. "Barkow, you hate me and you know it. If I ever leave that jail alive, it won't be your fault."

Barkow shrugged. "Think what you want," he said indifferently. "I believe in law and order. We've got a nice little community at Painted Rock and we want to keep it that way. Boyne had challenged you, and that was different. Bonaro had no part in the fight."

"No use arguin' that here," Gomer protested. "Court's the place for that. Let's go."

Tex Brisco lounged down the steps, his thumbs hooked in his belt. He stared at Gomer.

"I don't like you," he said coolly. "I don't like you a bit. I think you're yellow as a coyote. I think you bob ever' time this here Barkow says bob."

Gomer's face whitened, and his eyes shifted.

"You've got no call to start trouble!" he said. "I'm doin' my duty."

"Let it ride," Caradec told Tex. "There's plenty of time."

"Yeah," Tex drawled, his hard eyes on Gomer, "but just for luck I'm goin' to mount and trail you into town, keepin' to the hills. If that bunch of Shute riders gets fancy, I'm goin' to get myself a sheriff, and"—his eyes shifted—"mebbe another hombre."

"Is that a threat?" Barkow said contemptuously. "Talk is cheap."

"Want to see how cheap?" Tex prodded. His eyes were ugly and he was itching for a fight. It showed in every line of him. "Want me to make it expensive?"

Bruce Barkow was no fool. He had not seen Tex Brisco in action, yet there was something chill and deadly about the tall Texan. Barkow shrugged.

"We came here to enforce the law. Is this resistance, Caradec?"

"No," Rafe said. "Let's go."

The three men turned their horses and walked them down the trail toward Long Valley. Tex Brisco threw a saddle on his horse, and mounted. Glancing back, Pod Gomer saw the Texan turn his horse up a trail into the trees. He swore viciously.

Caradec sat his horse easily. The trouble would not come now. He was quite sure the plan had been to get him away, then claim the Shute riders had taken him from the law. Yet he was as sure it would not come to that now. Pod Gomer would know that Brisco's Winchester was within range. Also, Rafe was still wearing his guns.

Rafe rode warily, lagging a trifle behind the sheriff. He glanced at Barkow, but the rancher's face was expressionless. Ahead of them, in a tight bunch, waited the Shute riders.

The first he recognized were the Blazers. There was another man, known as Joe Gorman, whom he also recognized. Red Blazer started forward abruptly.

"He come, did he?" he shouted. "Now we'll show him!"

"Get back!" Gomer ordered sharply.

"Huh?" Red glared at Gomer. "Who says I'll get back! I'm stringin' this hombre to the first tree we get to!"

"You stay back!" Gomer ordered. "We're takin' this man in for trial!"

Red Blazer laughed. "Come on, boys!" he yelled. "Let's hang the skunk!"

"I wouldn't, Red," Rafe Caradec said calmly. "You've overlooked somethin'. I'm wearin' my guns. Are you faster than Trigger Boyne?"

Blazer jerked his horse's head around, his face pale but furious.

"Hey!" he yelled. "What the devil is this? I thought—"

"That you'd have an easy time of it?" Rafe shoved the black horse between Gomer and Barkow, pushing ahead of them. He rode right up to Blazer and let the big black shove into the other horse. "Well, get this Blazer! Any time you kill me, you'll do it with a gun in your hand, savvy? You're nothin' but a lot of lynch-crazy coyotes! Try it, damn it! Try it now, and I'll blow you out of that saddle so full of lead you'll sink a foot into the ground!"

Rafe's eyes swept the crowd.

"Think this is a joke? That goes for any of you! And as for Gomer, he knows, that if you hombres want any trouble he gets it too! There's a man up in the hills

68

with a Winchester, and if you don't think he can empty saddles, start somethin'. That Winchester carries sixteen shots and I've seen him empty it and get that many rabbits! I'm packing two guns. I'm askin' you now so if you want any of what I've got, start the ball rollin'. Mebbe you'd get me but I'm tellin' you there'll be more dead men around there than you can shake a stick at!"

Joe Gorman spoke quickly. "Watch it, boys! There is a hombre up on the mountain with a rifle! I seen him!"

"What the blue blazes is this?" Red Blazer repeated.

"The fun's over," Rafe replied shortly. "You might as well head for home and tell Dan Shute to kill his own wolves. I'm wearin' my guns and I'm goin' to keep 'em. I'll stand trial, but you know and I know that Bonaro got what he was askin' for." Caradec turned his eyes on Blazer. "As for you, stay out of my sight! You're too blasted willin' to throw your hemp over a man you think is helpless! I don't like skunks and never did!"

"You can't call me a skunk!" Blazer bellowed.

Rafe stared at him. "I just did," he said calmly.

VII

For a full minute their eyes held. Rafe's hand was on his thigh within inches of his gun. If it came to gun play now, he would be killed, but Blazer and Barkow would go down, too, and there would be others. He had not exaggerated when he spoke of Tex Brisco's rifle shooting. The man was a wizard with the gun.

Red Blazer was trapped. White to the lips, he stared at Rafe, and could see cold, certain death looking back at him. He could stand it no longer.

"Why don't some of you do somethin'?" he bellowed.

Joe Gorman spat. "You done the talkin', Red."

"The hell with it!"

Blazer swung his horse around, touched spurs to the animal, and raced off at top speed.

Bruce Barkow's hand hovered close to his gun. A quick draw, a shot, and the man would be dead. Just like that. His lips tightened, and his elbow crooked. Gomer grabbed his wrist.

"Don't Bruce! Don't! That hombre up there . . . Look!"

Barkow's head swung. Brisco was in plain sight, his rifle resting over the limb of a tree. At that distance, he could not miss. Yet he was beyond pistol range, and while some of the riders had rifles, they were out in the open without a bit of cover.

Barkow jerked his arm away and turned his horse toward town. Rafe turned the black and rode beside him.

He said nothing, but Barkow was seething at the big man's obvious contempt.

Rafe Caradec had outfaced the lot of them. He had made them look fools. Yet Barkow remembered as well as each of the riders remembered, that Rafe had fired but three shots in the street battle, that all the shots had scored, and two men had died.

When the cavalcade reached the National, Rafe turned to Pod Gomer.

"Get your court goin'," he said calmly. "We'll have this trial now."

"Listen here!" Gomer burst out, infuriated. "You can do things like that too often! We'll have court when we get blamed good and ready!"

"No," Rafe said, "you'll hold court this afternoon— now. You haven't got any calendar to interfere. I have business to attend to that can't wait, and I won't. You'll have your trial today, or I'll leave and you can come and get me."

"Who are you tellin' what to do?" Gomer said angrily. "I'll have you know . . ."

"Then you tell him, Barkow. Or does he take his orders from Shute? Call that judge of yours and let's get this over."

Bruce Barkow's lips tightened. He could see that Gene Baker and Ann Rodney were standing in the doorway of the store, listening.

"All right," Barkow said savagely. "Call him down here."

Not much later Judge Roy Gargan walked into the stage station and looked around. He was a tall, slightly stooped man with a lean, hangdog face and round eyes. He walked up to the table and sat down in the chair behind it. Bruce Barkow took a chair to one side where he could see the judge.

Noting the move, Rafe Caradec sat down where both men were visible. Barkow, nettled, shifted his chair irritably. He glanced up and saw Ann Rodney come in, accompanied by Baker and Pat Higley. He scowled again. Why couldn't they stay out of this?

Slowly, the hangers-on around town filed in. Joe Benson came in and sat down close to Barkow. They exchanged looks. Benson's questioning glance made Barkow furious. If they wanted so much done, why didn't someone do something beside him?

"I'll watch from here," drawled a voice.

Barkow's head came up. Standing in the window behind and to the right of the judge was Tex Brisco. At the same instant Barkow noted him, the Texan lifted a hand.

"Hi, Johnny! Glad to see you!"

Bruce Barkow's face went hard. Johnny Gill, and beside him, Bo Marsh. If anything rusty was pulled in this courtroom the place would be a shambles. Maybe Dan Shute was right after all. If they were going to be crooked, why not dry-gulch the fellow and get it over? All Barkow's carefully worked out plans to get Caradec had failed.

There had been three good chances. Resistance, that would warrant killing in attempting an arrest. Attempted escape, if he so much as made a wrong move. Or lynching by the Shute riders. At every point they had been outguessed.

Judge Gargan slammed a six-shooter on the table.

"Order!" he proclaimed. "Court's in session! Reckon I'll appoint a jury. Six men will do. I'll have Joe Benson, Tom Blazer, Sam Mawson, Doc Otto and—"

"Joe Benson's not eligible," Caradec interrupted.

Gargan frowned. "Who's runnin' this court?"

"Supposedly," Rafe said quietly, "the law. Supposedly, the interests of justice. Joe Benson was a witness to the shootin', so he'll be called on to give testimony."

"Who you tellin' how to run this court?" Gargan demanded belligerently.

"Doesn't the defendant even have a chance to defend himself?" Caradec asked gently. He glanced around

72

at the crowd. "I think you'll all agree that a man on trial for his life should have a chance to defend himself. That he should be allowed to call and question witnesses, and that he should have an attorney. But since the Court hasn't provided an attorney, and because I want to, I'll act for myself. Now"—he looked around— "the Judge picked three members of the jury. I'd like to pick out three more. I'd like Pat Higley, Gene Baker and Ann Rodney as members of the jury."

"What?" Gargan roared. "I'll have no woman settin' on no jury in my court! Why, of all the . . ."

Rafe said smoothly, "It kind of looks like Your Honor doesn't know the law in Wyoming. By an act approved in December 1869, the first territorial legislature granted equal rights to women. Women served on juries in Laramie in 1870, and one was servin' as justice of the peace that year."

Gargan swallowed and looked uncomfortable. Barkow sat up, started to say something, but before he could open his mouth, Caradec was speaking again.

"As I understand, the attorney for the state and the defense attorney usually select a jury. As the Court has taken it upon himself to appoint a jury, I was just suggestin' the names of three reputable citizens I respect. I'm sure none of these three can be considered friends of mine, sorry as I am to say it.

"Of course," he added, "if the Court objects to these three people—if there's somethin' about their characters I don't know, or if they are not good citizens, then I take back my suggestion." He turned to look at Bruce Barkow. "Or mebbe Mr. Barkow objects to Ann Rodney servin' on the jury?"

Barkow sat up, flushing. Suddenly, he was burning with rage. This whole thing had got out of hand. What had happened to bring this about? He was acutely conscious that Ann was staring at him, her eyes wide, a flush mounting in her cheeks at his hesitation.

"No!" he said violently. "No, of course not. Let her sit, but let's get this business started."

Pod Gomer was slumped in his chair, watching cynically. His eyes shifted to Barkow with a faintly curious expression. The planner and schemer had missed out on this trial. It had been his idea to condemn the man in public, then see to it that he was hanged.

"You're actin' as prosecutin' attorney?" Gargan asked Barkow.

The rancher got to his feet, cursing the thought that had given rise to this situation. That Rafe Caradec had won the first round he was unpleasantly aware. Somehow they had never contemplated any trouble on the score of the jury. In the few trials held thus far the judge had appointed the jury and there had been no complaint. All the cases had gone off as planned.

"Your Honor," he began, "and Gentlemen of the Jury. You all know none of us here are lawyers. This court is bein' held only so's we can keep law and order in this community, and that's the way it will be till the country is organized. This prisoner was in a gunfight with Lemuel Boyne, known as Trigger. Boyne challenged him—some of you know the reason for that—and Caradec accepted. In the fight out in the street, Caradec shot Boyne and killed him.

"In almost the same instant, he lifted his gun and shot Gee Bonaro, who was innocently watchin' the battle from his window. If a thing like this isn't punished, any gunfighter is apt to shoot anybody he don't like at any time, and nothin' done about it. We've all heard that Caradec claims Bonaro had a rifle and was about to shoot at him, which was a plumb good excuse, but a right weak one. We know this Caradec had words with Bonaro at the Emporium, and almost got into a fight then and there. I say Caradec is guilty of murder in the first degree, and should be hung."

Barkow turned his head and motioned to Red Blazer.

"Red, you get up there and tell the jury what you know."

Red strode up to the chair that was doing duty for a witness stand and slouched down in the seat. He was unshaven, and his hair was uncombed. He sprawled his legs out and stuck his thumbs in his belt. He rolled his quid in his jaws, and spat.

"I seen this here Caradec shoot Boyne," he said, "then he ups with his pistol and cut down on Bonaro, who was a standin' in the window, just a-lookin'."

"Did Bonaro make any threatening moves toward Caradec?"

"Him?" Red's eyes opened wide. "Shucks, no. Gee was just a standin' there. Caradec was afeerd of him, an' seen a chance to kill him and get plumb away."

Rafe looked thoughtfully at Barkow. "Is the fact that the witness was not sworn in the regular way in this court? Or is his conscience delicate on the subject of perjury?"

"Huh?" Blazer sat up. "What'd he say?"

Barkow flushed. "It hasn't usually been the way here, but—"

"Swear him in," Caradec said calmly, "and have him say under oath what he just said."

He waited until this was done, and then as Red started to get up Rafe motioned him back.

"I've got a few questions," he said.

"Huh?" Red demanded belligerently. "I don't have to answer no more questions."

"Yes, you do." Rafe's voice was quiet. "Get back on that witness stand!"

"Do I have to?" Blazer demanded of Barkow, who nodded.

If there had been any easy way out, he would have taken it, but there was none. He was beginning to look at Rafe Caradec with new eyes.

Rafe got up and walked over to the jury.

"Gentlemen," he said, "none of you know me well.

None of us, as Barkow said, know much about how court business should be handled. All we want to do is get at the truth. I know that all of you here are busy men. You're willin' and anxious to help along justice and the beginnin's of law hereabouts, and all of you are honest men. You want to do the right thing. Red Blazer has just testified that I shot a man who was makin' no threatenin' moves, that Bonaro was standing in a window, just watching."

Caradec turned around and looked at Blazer thoughtfully. He walked over to him, squatted on his haunches and peered into his eyes, shifting first to one side, then the other. Red Blazer's face flamed.

"What's the matter?" he blared. "You gone crazy?"

"No," Caradec said. "Just lookin' at your eyes. I was just curious to see what kind of eyes a man had who could see through a shingle roof and a ceilin'."

"Huh?" Blazer glared.

The jury sat up, and Barkow's eyes narrowed. The courtroom crowd leaned forward.

"Why, Red, you must have forgot," Rafe said. "You were in the National when I killed Boyne. You were standin' behind Joe Benson. You were the first person I saw when I looked around. You could see me, and you could see Boyne—but you couldn't see the second-story window across the street!"

Somebody whooped, and Pat Higley grinned.

"I reckon he's right," Pat said coolly. "I was standin' right alongside of Red."

"That's right!" somebody from back in the courtroom shouted. "Blazer tried to duck out without payin' for his drink and Joe Benson stopped him!"

Everybody laughed, and Blazer turned fiery red, glaring back into the room to see who the speaker was, and not finding him.

Rafe turned to Barkow and smiled.

"Have you got another witness?"

Despite herself, Ann Rodney found herself admiring Rafe Caradec's composure, his easy manner. Her curiosity was stirred. What manner of man was he? Where was he from? What background had he? Was he only a wanderer, or was he something more, something different? His language, aside from his characteristic Texas drawl, his manner, spoke of refinement, yet she knew of his gun skill as exhibited in the Boyne fight.

"Tom Blazer's my next witness," Barkow said. "Swear him in."

Tom Blazer, a hulking redhead even bigger than Red, took the stand. Animosity glared from his eyes.

"Did you see the shootin'?" Barkow asked.

"You're darned right I did!" Tom declared, staring at Rafe. "I seen it, and I wasn't inside no saloon! I was right out in the street!"

"Was Bonaro where you could see him?"

"He sure was!"

"Did he make any threatening moves?"

"Not any!"

"Did he lift a gun?"

"He sure didn't!"

"Did he make any move that would give an idea he was goin' to shoot?"

"Nope. Not any." As Tom Blazer answered each question he glared triumphantly at Caradec.

Barkow turned to the jury. "Well, there you are. I think that's enough evidence. I think . . ."

"Let's hear Caradec ask his questions," Pat Higley said. "I want both sides of this yarn."

Rafe got up and walked over to Tom Blazer, then looked at the judge. "Your Honor, I'd like permission to ask one question of a man in the audience. He can be sworn in or not, just as you say."

Gargan hesitated uncertainly. Always before, things had gone smoothly. Trials had been railroaded through, objections swept aside, and the wordless little ranchers or other objectors to the rule of Barkow and Shute

77

had been helpless. This time preparations should have been more complete. He didn't know what to do.

"All right," he said, his misgivings showing in his expression and tone.

Caradec turned and looked at a short, stocky man with a brown mustache streaked with gray. "Grant," he said, "what kind of a curtain have you got over that window above your harness and saddle shop?"

Grant looked up. "Why, it ain't rightly no curtain," he said frankly. "It's a blanket."

"You keep it down all the time? The window covered?"

"Uh-huh. Sure do. Sun gets in there otherwise, and makes the floor hot and she heats up the store thataway. Keepin' that window covered keeps her cooler."

"It was covered the day of the shootin'?"

"Shore was."

"Where did you find the blanket after the shootin'?"

"Well, she laid over the sill, partly inside, partly outside."

Rafe turned to the jury. "Miss Rodney and gentlemen, I believe the evidence is clear. The window was covered by a blanket. When Bonaro fell after I shot him, he tumbled across the sill, tearin' down the blanket. Do you agree?"

"Shore!" Gene Baker found his voice. The whole case was only too obviously a frameup to get Caradec. It was like Bonaro to try to sneak killing, anyway. "If that blanket hadn't been over the window, then he couldn't have fallen against it and carried part out with him!"

"That's right." Rafe turned on Tom Blazer. "Your eyes seem to be as amazin' as your brother's. You can see through a wool blanket!"

Blazer sat up with a jerk, his face dark with sullen rage. "Listen!" he said, "I'll tell you—"

"Wait a minute!" Rafe whirled on him, and thrust a finger in his face. "You're not only a perjurer but a thief! What did you do with that Winchester Bonaro dropped out of the window?"

"It wasn't no Winchester!" Blazer blared furiously. "It was a Henry!"

Then, seeing the expression on Barkow's face, and hearing the low murmur that swept the court, he realized what he had said. He started to get up, then sank back, angry and confused.

Rafe Caradec turned toward the jury.

"The witness swore that Bonaro had no gun, yet he just testified that the rifle Bonaro dropped was a Henry. Gentlemen and Miss Rodney, I'm goin' to ask that you recommend the case be dismissed, and also that Red and Tom Blazer be held in jail to answer charges of perjury!"

"What?" Tom Blazer came out of the witness chair with a lunge. "Jail? Me? Why, you—"

He leaped, hurling a huge red-haired fist in a roundhouse swing. Rafe Caradec stepped in with a left that smashed Blazer's lips, then a solid right that sent him crashing to the floor.

Rafe glanced at the judge. "And that, I think," he said quietly, "is contempt of court!"

Pat Higley got up abruptly. "Gargan, I reckon you better dismiss this case. You haven't got any evidence or anything that sounds like evidence, and I guess everybody here heard about Caradec facin' Bonaro down in the store. If he wanted to shoot him, there was his chance."

Gargan swallowed. "Case dismissed," he said.

He looked up at Bruce Barkow, but the rancher was walking toward Ann Rodney. She glanced at him, then her eyes lifted and beyond him she saw Rafe Caradec. How fine his face was! It was a rugged, strong face. There was character in it, and sincerity. . . .

She came down with a start. Bruce was speaking to her. "Gomer told me he had a case or I'd never have been a party to this. He's guilty as he can be, but he's smooth."

Ann looked down at Bruce Barkow, and suddenly his eyes looked different to her than ever before. "He may be guilty of a lot of things," she said tartly, "but if ever there was a cooked-up, dishonest case, it was this one. And everyone in town knew it! If I were you, Bruce Barkow, I'd be ashamed of myself!"

Abruptly she turned her back on him and started for the door, yet as she went she glanced up. For a brief instant her eyes met those of Rafe Caradec and something within her leaped. Her throat seemed to catch. Head high, she hurried past him into the street. The store seemed a long distance away.

VIII

When Bruce Barkow walked into Pod Gomer's office, the sheriff was sitting in his swivel chair. In the big leather armchair across the room Dan Shute was waiting.

He was a big man, with massive shoulders, powerfully muscled arms, and great hands. A shock of dusky blond hair covered the top of his head, and his eyebrows were the color of corn silk. He looked up as Barkow came in, and when he spoke his voice was rough. "You shore played hob!"

"The man's smart, that's all!" Barkow said. "Next time we'll have a better case."

"Next time?" Dan Shute lounged back in the big chair, the contempt in his eyes unconcealed. "There ain't goin' to be a next time. You're through, Barkow. From now on this is my show, and we run it my way. Caradec needs killin', and we'll kill him. Also, you're goin' to foreclose that mortgage on the Rodney place."

"No,"—he held up a hand as Barkow started to speak —"you wait. You was all for pullin' this slick stuff. Winnin' the girl, gettin' your property the easy way, the legal way. To blazes with that! This Caradec is makin' a monkey of you! You're not slick! You're just a country boy playin' with a real smooth lad!

"To blazes with that smooth stuff! You foreclose on that mortgage and do it plumb quick! I'll take care of

Mr. Rafe Caradec! With my own hands or guns if necessary. We'll clean that country down there so slick of his hands and cattle they won't know what happened!"

"That won't get it," Barkow protested. "You let me handle this. I'll take care of things!"

Dan Shute looked up at Barkow, his eyes sardonic. "I'll run this show. You're takin' the back seat, Barkow, from now on. All you've done is make us out fumblin' fools! Also," he added calmly, "I'm takin' over that girl."

"*What?*" Barkow whirled, his face livid. In his wildest doubts of Shute, and he had had many of them, this was one thing that had never entered his mind.

"You heard me," Shute replied. "She's a neat little lady, and I can make a place for her out to my ranch. You messed up all around, so I'm takin' over."

Barkow laughed, but his laugh was hollow, with something of fear in it. Always before Dan Shute had been big, silent and surly, saying little, but letting Barkow plan and plot and take the lead. Bruce Barkow had always thought of the man as a sort of strong-arm squad to use in a pinch. Suddenly he was shockingly aware that this big man was completely sure of himself, that he held him, Barkow, in contempt. He would ride roughshod over everything.

"Dan," Barkow protested, trying to keep his thoughts ordered, "you can't play with a girl's affections. She's in love with me! You can't do anything about that! You think she'd fall out of love with one man, and—"

Dan Shute grinned. "Who said anything about love? You talk about that all you want. Talk to yourself. I want the girl, and I'm goin' to have her. It doesn't make any difference who says no, and that goes for Gene Baker, her, or you."

Bruce Barkow stood flat-footed and pale. Suddenly he felt sick and empty. Here it was then. He was through. Dan Shute had told him off, in front of Pod

Gomer. Out of the tail of his eye he could see the calm, yet cynical expression on Gomer's face.

He looked up and felt small under the flat, ironic gaze of Shute's eyes. "All right, Dan, if that's the way you feel. I expect we'd better part company."

Shute chuckled. His voice was rough when he spoke. "No," he said, "we don't part company. You sit tight. You're holdin' that mortgage, and I want that land. You had a good idea there, Barkow, but you're too weak-kneed to swing it. I'll swing it. Mebbe if you're quiet and obey orders, I'll see you get some of it."

Bruce Barkow glared at Shute. For the first time he knew what hatred was. Here, in a few minutes, he had been destroyed. This story would go the rounds. Before nightfall everyone in town would know it.

Crushed, Barkow stared at Shute with hatred livid in his eyes. "You'll go too far!" he said viciously.

Shute shrugged. "You can live, an' come out of this with a few dollars," he said calmly, "or you can die. I'd just as soon kill you, Barkow." He picked up his hat. "We had a nice thing. That shanghaiin' idea was yours. Why you didn't shoot him, I'll never know. If you had, this Caradec would never have run into him at all, and would never have come in here, stirrin' things up. You could have foreclosed that mortgage, and we could be makin' a deal on that oil now."

"Caradec don't know anything about that," Barkow protested.

"Like sin he don't!" Dan Shute sneered. "Caradec's been watched by my men for days. He's been wise there was somethin' in the wind and he's scouted all over that place. Well, he was down to the knob the other day, and he took a long look at that oil seepage. He's no fool, Barkow."

Bruce Barkow looked up. "No," he replied suddenly, "he's not, and he's a hand with a gun, too. Dan! He's a hand with a gun! He took Boyne!"

Shute shrugged. "Boyne was nothin'! I could have

spanked him with his own gun. I'll kill Caradec some day, but first I want to beat him. To beat him with my own hands!"

He heaved himself out of the chair and stalked outside. For an instant, Barkow stared after him, then his gaze shifted to Pod Gomer.

The sheriff was absently whittling a small stick. "Well," he said, "he told you."

Hard and grim, Barkow's mouth tightened. So Gomer was in it, too. He started to speak, then hesitated. Like Caradec, Gomer was no fool, and he, too, was a good hand with a gun. Barkow shrugged. "Dan sees things wrong," he said. "I've still got an ace in the hole." He looked at Gomer. "I'd like it better if you were on my side."

Pod Gomer shrugged. "I'm with the winner. My health is good. All I need is more money."

"You think Shute's the winner?"

"Don't you?" Gomer asked. "He told you plenty, and you took it."

"Yes, I did, because I know I'm no match for him with a gun. Nor for you." He studied the sheriff thoughtfully. "This is goin' to be a nice thing, Pod. It would split well, two ways."

Gomer got up and snapped his knife shut. "You show me the color of some money," he said, "and Dan Shute out, and we might talk. Also," he added, "if you mention this to Dan, I'll call you a liar in the street or in the National. I'll make you use that gun.

"I won't talk," Barkow said. "Only, I've been learnin' a few things. When we get answers to some of the messages you sent, and some I sent, we should know more. Borger wouldn't let Caradec off that ship willin'ly after he knew Rodney. I think he deserted. I think we can get something on him for mutiny, and that means hangin'!"

"Mebbe you can," Gomer agreed. "You show me you're holdin' good cards, and I'll back you to the limit."

Bruce Barkow walked out on the street and watched Pod Gomer's retreating back. Gomer, at least, he understood. He knew the man had no use for him, but if he could show evidence that he was to win, then Gomer would be a powerful ally. Judge Gargan would go as Gomer went, and would always adopt the less violent means.

The cards were on the table now. Dan Shute was running things. What he would do, Barkow was not sure. He realized suddenly, with no little trepidation, that after all his association with Shute he knew little of what went on behind the hard brutality of the rancher's face. Yet he was not a man to lag or linger. What he did would be sudden, brutal, and thorough, but it would make a perfect shield under which he, Barkow, could operate and carry to fulfillment his own plans.

Dan Shute's abrupt statement of his purpose in regard to Ann Rodney had jolted Barkow. Somehow, he had taken Ann for granted. He had always planned a marriage. That he wanted her land was true. Perhaps better than Shute he knew what oil might mean in the future, for Barkow was a farsighted man. But Ann Rodney was lovely and interesting. She would be a good wife for him. There was one way he could defeat Dan Shute on that score. To marry Ann at once.

True, it might precipitate a killing, but already Bruce Barkow was getting ideas on that score. He was suddenly less disturbed about Rafe Caradec than Dan Shute. The rancher loomed large and formidable in his mind. He knew the brutality of the man, had seen him kill, and knew with what coldness he regarded people or animals.

Bruce Barkow made up his mind. Come what may, he was going to marry Ann Rodney.

He could, he realized, marry her and get her clear away from here. His mind leaped ahead. Flight to the northwest to the gold camps would be foolhardy. To the Utah country would be as bad. In either case, Shute might and probably would overtake him. There remained another way out, and one that Shute probably would never suspect—he could strike for Fort Phil Kearney not far distant. Then, with or without a scouting party for escort, they could head across country and reach the Yellowstone. Or he might even try the nearer Powder River.

A steamer had ascended the Yellowstone earlier that year, and there was every chance that another would come. If not, with a canoe or barge they could head downstream until they encountered such a boat and buy passage to St. Louis.

Ann and full title to the land would be in his hands then. He could negotiate a sale or the leasing of the land from a safe distance. The more he thought of this, the more he was positive it remained the only solution for him.

Let Gomer think what he would. Let Dan Shute believe him content with a minor role. He would go ahead with his plans, then strike suddenly and swiftly and be well on his way before Shute realized what had happened. Once he made the Fort, he would be in the clear. Knowing the officers as well as he did, he was sure he could get an escort to the river.

He had never seen the Yellowstone, nor did he know very much about either that river or Powder River. But they had been used by many men as a high road to the West. He would use a river as an escape to the East.

Carefully he considered the plan. There were preparations to be made. Every angle must be considered. At his ranch were enough horses. He would borrow Baker's buckboard to take Ann for a ride, then at his ranch, they would mount and be off. With luck they would be well on their way before anyone so much as guessed what had happened.

Stopping by the store, he bought ammunition from

Baker. He glanced up to find the storekeeper's eyes studying him, and he didn't like the expression.

"Is Ann in?" he asked.

Baker nodded, and jerked a thumb toward the curtain. Turning, Baker walked behind the curtain and looked at Ann, who arose as he entered. Quickly he sensed a coolness that had not been there before. This was no time to talk of marriage. First things first.

He shrugged shamefacedly. "I suppose you're thinkin' pretty bad of me," he suggested ruefully. "I know now I shouldn't have listened to Dan Shute or to Gomer. Pod swore he had a case, and Shute claims Caradec is a crook and a rustler. If I had known I wouldn't have had any hand in it."

"It was pretty bad," Ann agreed as she sat down and began knitting. "What will happen now?"

"I don't know," he admitted, "but I wish I could spare you all this. Before it's over I'm afraid there'll be more killin's and trouble. Dan Shute is plenty roused up. He'll kill Caradec."

She looked at him. "You think that will be easy?"

Surprised, he nodded. "Yes. Dan's a dangerous man, cruel and brutal. He's fast with a gun, too."

"I thought you were a friend of Dan Shute?" she asked, looking at him hard. "What's changed you, Bruce?"

He shrugged. "Oh, little things. He showed himself up today. He's brutal, unfeelin'. He'll stop at nothin' to gain his ends."

"I think he will," Ann said composedly. "I think he'll stop at Rafe Caradec."

Barkow stared at her. "Caradec seems to have impressed you. What makes you think that?"

"I never really saw him until today, Bruce," she admitted. "Whatever his motives, he is shrewd and capable. I think he is much more dangerous than Dan Shute. There's something behind him, too. He has background. I could see it in his manner more than his words. I wish I knew more about him."

Nettled at her defense of the man, and her apparent respect for him, Bruce shrugged his shoulders. "Don't forget, he probably killed your father."

She looked up. "Did he, Bruce?"

Her question struck fear from him. Veiling his eyes, he shrugged again. "You never know." He got up. "I'm worried about you, Ann. This country is going to be flamin' within a little while. If it ain't the fight here, it'll be the Indians. I wish I could get you out of it."

"But this is my home!" Ann protested. "It is all I have!"

"Not quite all." Her eyes fell before his gaze. "Ann, how would you like to go to St. Louis?"

She looked up, startled. "To St. Louis? But how—"

"Not so loud!" He glanced apprehensively at the door. There was no telling who might be listening. "I don't want anybody to know about it unless you decide and until we're gone. But, Ann, we *could* go. I've always wanted to marry you. There's no time better than now."

She got up and walked to the window. St. Louis. It was another world. She hadn't seen a city in six years. After all, they had been engaged for several months now.

"How would we get there?" she asked, turning to face him.

"That's a secret!" He laughed. "Don't tell anybody about it, but I've got a wonderful trip planned for you. I always wanted to do things for you, Ann. We could go away and be married within a few hours."

"Where?"

"By the chaplain at the Fort. One of the officers would stand up with me. There are a couple of officers' wives there, too."

"I don't know, Bruce," she said hesitantly. "I'll have to think about it."

He smiled and kissed her lightly. "Then think fast, honey. I want to get you away from all this trouble—and quick."

When he got outside in the street, he paused, smiling with satisfaction. "I'll show that Dan Shute a thing or two!" he told himself grimly. Abruptly, he turned toward the cabin where he lived.

Dan Shute, who had been leaning against the door of the building next door, straightened thoughtfully and snapped his cigarette into the dust. He had seen the satisfied smile on Barkow's face and knew he had been inside for some time. Shute stood on the boardwalk, staring into the dust. Big hands on his hips above the heavy guns, his gray hat pulled low, a stubble of corn-white beard along his hard jaws. "I think," he said to himself, looking up, "that I'll kill Bruce Barkow!" He added, "And I'm goin' to like the doin' of it!"

IX

GENE BAKER was sweeping his store and the stoop in front of it when he saw a tight little cavalcade of horsemen trot around the corner into the street. It was the morning after the fiasco of the trial. He had been worried and irritated while wondering what the reaction would be from Barkow and Shute. Then word had come to him of the break between the two at Gomer's office.

Dan Shute, riding a powerful gray, was in the van of the bunch of horsemen. He rode up to the stoop of Baker's store and reined in. Behind him were Red and Tom Blazer, Joe Gorman, Fritz Handl, "Fats" McCabe and others of the hard bunch that trailed with Shute.

"Gene," Shute said abruptly, resting his big hands on the pommel of the saddle, "don't sell any more supplies to Caradec or any of his crowd." He added harshly, "I'm not askin' you. I'm tellin' you. If you do, I'll put you out of business and run you out of the country. You know I don't make threats. The chances are Caradec won't be alive by daybreak anyway—but just in case, you've been told!"

Without giving Baker a chance to reply, Dan Shute touched spurs to his horse and led off down the south trail toward the Crazy Woman.

The door slammed behind Baker. "Where are they going?" Ann wanted to know. "What are they going to do?"

Gene stared after them bleakly. This was the end of something. "They are goin' after Caradec and his crowd, Ann."

"What will they do to him?"

Something inside her went sick and frightened. She had always been afraid of Dan Shute. The way he looked at her made her shrink. He was the only human being of whom she had ever been afraid. He seemed without feeling, without decency, without regard for anything but his own immediate desires.

"Kill him," Baker said. "They'll kill him. Shute's a hard man, and that's a mighty wicked gang."

"But can't someone warn him?" Ann protested.

Baker glanced at her. "So far as we know, Caradec is a crook and mebbe a killer, Ann. You ain't gettin' soft on him, are you?"

"No!" she exclaimed, startled. "Of course not! What an idea! Why, I've scarcely talked to him!" Yet there was a heavy, sinking feeling in her heart as she watched the riders disappear in the dust along the southward trail. If there was only something she could do! If she could warn them!

Suddenly she remembered the bay horse her father had given her. Because of the Indians, she had not been riding in a long time, but if she took the mountain trail. . . .

Hurrying through the door she swiftly saddled the bay. There was no thought in her mind. She was acting strictly on impulse, prompted by some memory of the way the hair swept back from Rafe's brow, and the look in his eyes when he met her gaze. She told herself she wanted to see no man killed, that Bo Marsh and Johnny Gill were her friends. Yet even in her heart she knew the excuse would not do. She was thinking of Rafe, and only of Rafe.

The bay was in fine shape and impatient after his long restraint in the corral. He started for the trail, eagerly, and his ears pricked up at every sound. The leaves had turned to red and gold now and the air held a hint of frost. Winter was coming. Soon the country would be blanketed, inches deep, under a thick covering of snow.

Hastily Ann's mind leaped ahead. The prairie trail, which the Shute riders had taken, swept wide into the valley, then crossed the Crazy Woman and turned to follow the stream up the canyon. By cutting across over the mountain trail there was every chance she could beat them to the ranch. In any case, her lead would be slight due to the start the bunch had.

The trail crossed the mountainside through a long grove of quaking aspens, their leaves shimmering in the cool wind, dark green above, gray below. Now, with oncoming autumn most of the leaves had turned to bright yellow intermixed with crimson. Here and there among the forest of mounting color were the darker arrowheads of spruce and lodgepole pine.

Once, coming out in a small clearing, she got a view of the valley below. She had gained a little, but only a little. Frightened, she touched spurs to the bay and the little horse leaped ahead and swept down through the woods at a rapid gallop.

Ahead, there was a ledge. It was a good six miles off yet, but from there she could see the canyon of the Crazy Woman and the upper canyon. A rider had told her that Caradec had been putting up hay in the wind-sheltered upper canyon and was obviously planning on feeding his stock there by the warm spring.

She recalled it because she remembered it was something her father had spoken of doing. There was room in the upper valley for many cattle. If there was hay enough for them, the warm water would be a help, and with only a little such the cattle could survive even the coldest winter.

Fording the stream where Caradec had encountered the young squaw, she rode higher on the mountain, angling across the slope under a magnificent stand of lodgepole pine. It was a splendid avenue of trees, all seemingly of the same size and shape, as though cast from a mold.

Once she glimpsed a deer, and another time in the distance in a small, branching valley she saw a small bunch of elk. This was her country. No wonder her father had loved it, wanted it, worked to get and to keep it.

Had he paid the mortgage? But why wouldn't Bruce have told her if he had? She could not believe him dishonest and deceitful. Certainly he had made no effort to foreclose, but had been most patient and thoughtful with her.

What would he think of this ride to warn a man he regarded as an enemy? She could not sit idly by and know men were about to be killed. She would never forgive herself if she had made no effort to avert it.

Too often she had listened to her father discourse on the necessity for peace and consideration of others. She believed in that policy wholeheartedly. The fact that occasionally violence was necessary did not alter her convictions one whit. No system of philosophy or ethics, no growth of government, no improvement in living came without trial and struggle. Struggle, she had often heard her father say, was the law of growth.

Without giving too much thought to it, she understood that such men as Rafe Caradec, Trigger Boyne, Tex Brisco and others of their ilk were needed. For all their violence, their occasional heedlessness and their desire to go their own way, they were men building a new world in a rough and violent land where everything tended to extremes. Mountains were high, the prairies wide, the streams roaring, the buffalo by the thousand and tens of thousand. It was a land where nothing was small, nothing was simple. Everything, the lives of men and the stories they told, ran to extremes.

The bay pony trotted down the trail, then around a

stand of lodgepole. Ann brought him up sharply on the lip of the ledge that had been her first goal.

Below her, a vast and magnificent panorama, lay the ranch her father had pioneered. The silver curve of the Crazy Woman lay below and east of her, and opposite her ledge was the mighty wall of the canyon. From below, a faint thread of smoke among the trees marked the cabin.

Turning her head she looked west and south into the upper canyon. Far away, she seemed to see a horseman moving and the black dot of a herd. Turning the bay she started west, riding fast. If they were working the upper canyon she still had a chance.

An hour later, the little bay showing signs of his rough traveling, she came down to the floor of the canyon. Not far away, she could see Rafe Caradec moving a bunch of cattle into the trees.

He looked around at her approach, and the black, flat-crowned hat came off his head. His dark wavy hair was plastered to his brow with sweat, and his eyes were gray and curious.

"Good mornin'!" he said. "This is a surprise!"

"Please!" she burst out. "This isn't a social call! Dan Shute's riding this way with twenty men or more. He's going to wipe you out!"

Rafe's eyes sharpened. "You sure?" She could see the quick wonder in his eyes at her warning, then he wheeled his horse and yelled, "Johnny! Johnny Gill! Come a-runnin'!"

Jerking his rifle from his boot, he looked at her again. He put his hand over hers suddenly, and she started at his touch.

"Thanks, Ann," he said simply. "You're regular!"

Then he was gone, and Johnny Gill was streaking after him. As Gill swept by, he lifted a hand and waved.

There they went. Below were twenty men, all armed. Would they come through alive? She turned the bay and, letting the pony take his own time, started him back over the mountain trail.

Rafe Caradec gave no thought to Ann's reason for warning him. There was no time for that. Tex Brisco and Bo Marsh were at the cabin. They were probably working outside, and their rifles would probably be in the cabin and beyond them. If they were cut off from their guns, the Shute riders would mow them down and kill them one by one at long range with rifle fire.

Rafe heard Gill coming up, and slacked off a little to let the little cowhand draw alongside. "Shute!" he said. "And about twenty men. I guess this is the payoff!"

"Yeah!" Gill yelled.

Rifle fire came to them suddenly. A burst of shots, then a shot that might have been from a pistol. Their horses rounded the entrance and raced down the main canyon toward the cabin on the Crazy Woman, running neck and neck. A column of smoke greeted them, and they could see riders circling and firing.

"The trees on the slope!" Rafe yelled and raced for them.

He reached the trees with the black at a dead run and hit the ground before the animal had ceased to move. He raced to the rocks at the edge of the trees. His rifle lifted, settled, his breath steadied, and the rifle spoke.

A man shouted and waved an arm, and at the same moment, Gill fired. A horse went down. Two men, or possibly three, lay sprawled in the clearing before the cabin.

Were Tex and Bo already down? Rafe steadied himself and squeezed off another shot. A saddle emptied. He saw the fallen man lunge to his feet, then spill over on his face. Coolly then, taking their time, he and Gill began to fire. Another man went down, and rifles began to smoke in their direction. A bullet clipped the leaves overhead but too high.

Rafe knocked the hat from a man's head. As the fellow sprinted for shelter, he dropped him. Suddenly the attack broke. He saw the horses sweeping away from them in a ragged line. Mounting, Rafe and Gill rode cautiously toward the cabin.

There was no cabin. There was only a roaring inferno of flames. There were five sprawled bodies, and Rafe ran toward them. A Shute rider—another. Then he saw Bo.

The boy was lying on his face with a dark, spreading stain on the back of his shirt. There was no sign of Tex.

Rafe dropped to his knees and put a hand over the young cowhand's heart. It was still beating!

Gently, with Johnny lending a hand, he turned the boy over. Then, working with the crude but efficient skill picked up in war and struggle in a half-dozen countries, he examined the wounds.

"Four times!" he said grimly. Suddenly, he felt something mount and swell within him, a tide of fierce, uncontrollable anger!

Around one bullet hole in the stomach the cloth of the cowhand's shirt was smoldering!

"I seen that!" It was Tex Brisco, his face haggard and smoke grimed. "I seen it! I know who done it! He walked up while the kid was layin' there and stuck a gun against his stomach and shot! He didn't want the kid to go quick; he wanted him to die slow and hard!"

"Who done it?" Gill demanded fiercely. "I'll git him now! Right now!"

Brisco's eyes were red and inflamed. "Nobody gets him but me. This kid was your pard, but I *seen* it!" He turned abruptly on Rafe. "Boss, let me go to town. I want to kill me a man!"

"It won't do, Tex," Caradec said quietly. "I know how you feel, but the town will be full of 'em. They'll be celebratin'. They burned our cabin, ran off some cattle, and they got Bo. It wouldn't do!"

"Yeah," Tex spat. "I know. But they won't be expectin' any trouble now. If you don't let me go, I'll quit!"

Rafe looked up from the wounded man. "All right, Tex, I told you I know how you feel. But if somethin' should happen—who did it?"

"Tom Blazer! That big redhead. He always hated the kid. Shute shot the kid down and left him lay. I was out back in the woods lookin' for a pole to cut. They rode up so fast the kid never had a chance. He was hit twice before he knew what was goin' on. Hit again when he started toward the house. After the house was afire, Tom Blazer walked up, and the kid was conscious. Tom said somethin' to Bo, shoved the gun against him, and pulled the trigger."

He stared miserably at Bo. "I was out of pistol range. Took me a few minutes to get closer, then I got me two men before you rode up." Wheeling, he headed toward the corral.

Rafe had stopped the flow of blood, and Johnny had returned with a blanket from a line back of the house. "Reckon we better get him over in the trees, Boss," Gill said.

Easing the cowboy to the blanket with care, Rafe and Johnny carried Bo into the shade in a quiet place under the pines. Caradec glanced up as they put him down. Tex Brisco was riding out of the canyon. Johnny Gill watched him go.

"Boss," Gill said, "I wanted like blazes to go, but I ain't the man Brisco is. Rightly, I'm a quiet man, but that Texan is a wolf on the prowl. I'm some glad I'm not Tom Blazer right now!"

He looked down at Bo Marsh. The young cowhand's face was flushed, his breathing hoarse.

"Will he live, Rafe?" Johnny asked softly.

Caradec shrugged. "I don't know," he said honestly. "He needs better care than I can give him." He studied the situation thoughtfully. "Johnny," he said, "you stay

97

with him. Better take time to build a lean-to over him in case of rain or snow. Get some fuel, too."

"What about you?" Johnny asked. "Where you goin'?"

"To the Fort. There's an Army doctor there. I'll go get him."

"Reckon he'll come this far?" Johnny asked doubtingly.

"He'll come!"

Rafe Caradec mounted the black and rode slowly away into the dusk. It was a long ride to the Fort. Even if he got the doctor it might be too late. That was a chance he would have to take. There was small danger of an attack now.

Yet it was not a return of Dan Shute's riders that disturbed him, but a subtle coolness in the air, a chill that was of more than autumn. Winters in this country could be bitterly cold. All the signs gave evidence this one would be the worst in years, and now they were without a cabin. He rode on toward the Fort, with a thought that Tex Brisco now must be nearing town.

X

It was growing late. Painted Rock lay swathed in velvety darkness when Tex Brisco walked his horse down to the edge of town. He stopped across the bend of the stream from town and left his horse among the trees there. He would have a better chance to escape from across the stream than from the street. By leaving town on foot, he could create some doubt as to his whereabouts.

He was under no misapprehension as to the problem he faced. Painted Rock would be filled to overflowing with Shute and Barkow riders, many of whom knew him by sight. Yet though he could vision their certainty of victory, their numbers, and was well aware of the reckless task he had chosen, he knew they would not be expecting him or any riders from Crazy Woman.

He tied his horse loosely to a bush among the trees and crossed the stream on a log. Once across, he thought of his spurs. Kneeling down, he unfastened them from his boots and hung them over a root near the end of the log. He wanted no jingling spurs to give his presence away at an inopportune moment.

Carefully avoiding any lighted dwellings, he made his way through the scattered houses to the back of the row of buildings along the street. He was wearing the gun he usually wore. For luck he had taken another one from his saddlebags and thrust it into his waist band.

Tex Brisco was a man of the frontier. From riding

the range in south and west Texas, he had drifted north with trail herds. He had seen some of the wild days of Dodge and Ellsworth, some hard fighting down in the Nations, and with rustlers along the Border.

He was an honest man, a sincere man. He had a quality to be found in many men of his kind and period —a sense of deep-seated loyalty that was his outstanding trait.

Hard and reckless in demeanor, he rode with dash and acted with a flair. He had at times been called a hardcase. Yet no man lived long in a dangerous country if he were reckless. There was a place always for courage, but intelligent courage, not the heedlessness of a harebrained youngster.

Tex Brisco was twenty-five years old, but he had been doing a man's work since he was eleven. He had walked with men, ridden with men, fought with men as one of them. He had asked no favors and been granted none. Now, at twenty-five, he was a seasoned veteran. He was a man who knew the plains and the mountains, knew cattle, horses, and guns.

Shanghaied, he had quickly seen that the sea was not his element. He had concealed his resentment and gone to work, realizing that safety lay along that route. He had known his time would come. It had come when Rafe Caradec came aboard, and all his need for friendship, for loyalty and for a cause had been tied to the big, soft-spoken stranger.

Now Painted Rock was vibrant with danger. The men who did not hate him in Painted Rock were men who would neither speak for him nor act for him. It was like Tex Brisco that he did not think in terms of help. He had his job, he knew his problem, and he knew he was the man to do it.

The National Saloon was booming with sound. The tinny jangle of an out-of-tune piano mingled with hoarse laughter, shouts, and the rattle of glasses. The hitching rail was lined with horses.

Tex walked between the buildings to the edge of the dark and empty street. Then he walked up to the horses and, speaking softly, made his way along the hitching rail, turning every slipknot into a hard knot.

The Emporium was dark except for a light in Baker's living quarters where he sat with his wife and Ann Rodney.

The stage station was lighted by the feeble glow of a light over a desk as the station agent worked late over his books.

It was a moonless night and the stars were bright. Tex lit a cigarette, loosened his guns in his holsters, and studied the situation. The National was full. To step into that saloon would be suicide. Tex had no such idea in mind. It was early; he would have to wait. Yet might it not be the best way, if he stepped in? There would be a moment of confusion. In that instant he could act.

Working his way back to a window, he studied the interior. It took him several minutes to locate Tom Blazer. The big man was standing by the bar with Fats McCabe. Slipping to the other end of the window, Tex could see that no one was between them and the rear door.

He stepped back into the darkest shadows. Leaning against the building, he finished his cigarette. When it was down to a stub, he threw it on the ground and carefully rubbed it out with the toe of his boot. Then he pulled his hat low and walked around to the rear of the saloon.

There was some scrap lumber there. He skirted the rough pile, avoiding some bottles. It was cool out here. He rubbed his fingers, working his hands to keep the circulation going. Then he stepped up to the door and turned the knob. It opened under his hand. If it made a sound, it went unheard.

Stepping inside, he closed the door after him, pleased that it opened outward.

In the hurly-burly of the interior one more cowhand went unseen. Nobody even glanced his way. He sidled up the bar, then reached over under Tom Blazer's nose, drew the whisky bottle toward him, and poured a drink into a glass just rinsed by the bartender.

Tom Blazer scarcely glanced at the bottle for other bottles were being passed back and forth. Fats Mc-Cabe stood beside Tom, and without noticing Tex, went on talking.

"That blasted Marsh!" Tom said thickly. "I got him! I been wantin' him a long time! You should have seen the look in his eyes when I shoved that pistol against him and pulled the trigger!"

Tex's lips tightened, and he poured his glass full once more. He left it sitting on the bar in front of him.

His eyes swept the room. Dan Shute was not here and that worried him. He would have felt better to have had the rancher under his eyes. Bruce Barkow was here, though, and Pod Gomer. Tex moved over a little closer to McCabe.

"That'll finish 'em off!" McCabe was saying. "When Shute took over I knew they wouldn't last long! If they get out of the country, they'll be lucky. They've no supplies left. It will be snowin' within a few days. The winter will get 'em if we don't, or the Injuns."

Tex Brisco smiled grimly. *Not before I get you!* he thought. *That comes first.*

The piano was banging away with *Oh, Susanna!* and a bunch of cowhands were trying to sing. Joe Benson leaned on his bar talking to Pod Gomer. Barkow sat at a table in the corner, staring morosely into a glass. Joe Gorman and Fritz Handl were watching a poker game.

Tex glanced again at the back door. No one stood between the door and himself. Well, why wait?

Just then, Tom Blazer reached for the bottle in front of Tex, and Tex pulled it away from his hand.

Tom stared. "Hey, what you tryin' to do?" he demanded belligerently.

"I've come for you, Blazer," Tex said. "I've come to kill a skunk that shoots a helpless man when he's on his back. How are you against standin' men, Blazer?"

"Huh?" Tom Blazer said stupidly.

Then he realized what had been said, and thrust his big face forward for a closer look. The gray eyes he saw were icy, the lantern-jawed Texan's face was chill as death, and Tom Blazer jerked back. Slowly, his face white, Fats McCabe drew aside.

To neither man came the realization that Tex Brisco was alone. All they felt was the shock of his sudden appearance, here, among them.

Brisco turned, stepping one step away from the bar.

"Well, Tom," he said quietly, his voice just loud enough to carry over the sound of the music, "I've come for you."

Riveted to the spot, Tom Blazer felt an instant of panic. Brisco's presence here had the air of magic. Tom was half frightened by the sheer unexpectedness of it.

Sounds in the saloon seemed to die out, although they still went full blast. Tom stared across that short space like a man in a trance, trapped and faced with a fight to the death. There would be no escaping this issue, he knew. He might win and he might lose, but it was here, now, and he had to face it. He realized suddenly that it was a choice he had no desire to make.

Wouldn't anyone notice? Why didn't Fats say something? Tex Brisco stood there, staring at him.

"You've had your chance," Tex said gently. "Now I'm goin' to kill you!"

The shock of the word *kill* snapped Tom Blazer out of it. He dropped into a half crouch, and his lips curled in a snarl of mingled rage and fear. His clawed hand swept back for his gun.

In the throbbing rattle of the room the guns boomed like a crash of thunder. Heads whirled. Liquor-befuddled brains tried to focus eyes. All they saw was Tom Blazer sagging back against the bar, his shirt darkening with blood. The strained, foolish expression on his face was like that of a man who had been shocked beyond reason.

Facing the room was a lean, broad-shouldered man with two guns. As they looked, he swung a gun at Fats McCabe.

Instinctively, at the boom of guns, McCabe's brain reacted, but a shade too slow. His hand started for his gun. It was an involuntary movement that had he had but a moment's thought would never have been made. He had no intention of drawing. All he wanted was out, but the movement of his hand was enough. It was too much.

Tex Brisco's gun boomed again, and Fats toppled over on his face. Then Tex opened up. Three shots, blasting into the brightly lighted room, brought it to complete darkness. Brisco faded into that darkness, swung the door open, and vanished as a shot clipped the air over his head.

He ran hard for fifty feet, then ducked into the shadow of a barn, threw himself over a low corral fence and ran across the corral in a low crouch. Shouts and orders, then a crash of glass came from the saloon.

The door burst open again, and he could have got another man, but only by betraying his position. He crawled through the fence. Keeping close to a dark house, he ran swiftly to its far corner. He paused there, breathing heavily. So far, so good.

From here on he would be in comparative light, but the distance was enough now. He ran on swiftly for the river. Behind him he heard curses and yells as men found their knotted bridle reins. At the end of the log, Tex retrieved his spurs. Gasping for breath from his hard run, he ran across the log and started for his horse.

He saw it suddenly, and then saw something else.

In the dim light, Tex recognized Joe Gorman by his hat. Joe wore his hat brim rolled to a point in front.

"Hi, Texas!" Gorman said. Tex could see the gun in his hand, waist high and leveled on him.

"Hi, Joe. Looks like you smelled somethin'."

"Yeah,"—Joe nodded—"I did at that. I live in one of those houses over there with some of the other boys. Happened to see somebody ride up here in the dark and got curious. When you headed for the saloon, I got around you and went in. Then I saw you come in the back door. I slipped out just before the shootin' started so's I could beat you back here in case you got away."

"Too bad you missed the fun," Brisco said quietly.

Behind him the pursuit seemed to have gained no direction as yet. His mind was on a hair trigger, watching for a break. Which of his guns was still loaded? He had forgotten whether he had put the loaded gun in the holster or in his belt.

"Who'd you get?" asked Gorman.

"Tom Blazer. Fats McCabe, too."

"I figgered Tom. I told him he shouldn't have shot the kid. That was a low-down trick. But why shoot Fats?"

"He acted like he was reachin' for a gun."

"Huh! Don't take a lot to get a man killed, does it?"

Brisco could see in the dark enough to realize that Gorman was smiling a little.

"How do you want it, Tex? I let you have it now, or save you for Shute? He's a bad man, Tex."

"I think you'd better slip your gun in your holster and walk back home, Joe," Tex said. "You're the most decent one of a bad lot."

"Mebbe I want the money I'd get for you, Tex. I can use some."

"Think you'd live to collect?"

"You mean Caradec? He's through, Brisco. Through. We got Bo. Now we got you. That leaves only Caradec and Johnny Gill. They won't be so tough."

"You're wrong, Joe," Tex said quietly. "Rafe could

take the lot of you, and will. But you bought into my game yourself; I wouldn't ask for help, Joe. I'd kill you myself."

"You?" Gorman chuckled with real humor. "And me with the drop on you? Not a chance! Why, Tex *one* of these slugs would get you. If I have to start blastin', I'm goin' to empty the gun before I quit."

"Uh-huh," Tex agreed, "you might get me. But I'll get you, too."

Joe Gorman was incredulous. "You mean, get me before I could shoot?" He repeated, "Not a chance!"

The sounds of pursuit were coming closer. The men had a light now, and had found his tracks. "Toward the river, I'll be a coon!" a voice yelled. "Let's go!"

Here it was! Joe Gorman started to yell, then saw the black figure ahead of him move and his gun blaze. Tex felt the shocking jolt of a slug. His knees buckled, but his gun was out and he triggered two shots, fast. Joe started to fall, and he fired again, but the hammer fell on an empty chamber.

Tex jerked the slipknot in his reins loose and dragged himself into the saddle. He was bleeding badly. His mind felt hazy, but he saw Joe Gorman move on the ground, and heard him say, "You did it, damn you! You did it!"

"So long, Joe!" Tex whispered hoarsely.

He walked the horse for twenty feet, then started moving faster. His brain was singing with a strange noise, and his blood seemed to drum in his brains. He headed up the tree-covered slope, and the numbness crawled up his legs. He fought like a cornered wolf against the darkness that crept over him.

"I can't die—I can't!" he kept thinking. "Rafe'll need help! I can't!"

Fighting the blackness and numbness, he tied the bridle reins to the saddle-horn and thrust both feet clear through the stirrups. Sagging in the saddle, he got his handkerchief out and fumbled a knot, tying his wrists to the saddle-horn.

The light glowed and died. The horse walked on, weaving through a world of agony and soft clutching hands that seemed to b₃ pulling Tex down, pulling him down.

The darkness closed in around him, but under him he seemed still to feel the slow plodding of the horse. . . .

XI

ROUGHLY, the distance to the Fort was seventy miles. Rafe Caradec rode steadily into the increasing cold of the wind. There was no mistaking the seriousness of Bo's condition. The young cowhand was badly shot up, weak from loss of blood. Despite the amazing vitality of frontier men, his chance was slight unless his wounds had proper care.

Bowing his head to the wind, Rafe headed the horse down a draw and its partial shelter. There was no use thinking of Tex. Whatever had happened in Painted Rock had happened now. Brisco might be dead. He might be alive and safe, even now heading back to the Crazy Woman—or he might be wounded and in need of help.

Tex Brisco was an uncertainty but Bo Marsh hung between life and death, hence there was no choice.

The friendship and understanding between the lean, hard-faced Texan and Rafe Caradec had grown aboard ship. And Rafe was not one to take lightly the Texan's loyalty in joining him in his foray into Wyoming. Now Brisco might be dead, killed in a fight he would never have known but for Rafe. Yet Tex would have had it no other way. His destinies were guided by his loyalties. Those loyalties were his life, his religion, his reason for living.

Yet despite his worries over Marsh and Brisco, Rafe found his thoughts returning again and again to Ann

Rodney. Why had she ridden to warn them of the impending attack? Had it not been for that warning the riders would have wiped out Brisco at the same time they got Marsh, and would have followed it up to find Rafe and Johnny back in the canyon. It would have been, or could have been, a clean sweep.

Why had Ann warned them? Was it because of her dislike of violence and killing? Or was there some other, some deeper feeling?

Yet how could that be? What feeling could Ann have for any of them, believing as she seemed to believe that he was a thief or worse? The fact remained that she had come, that she had warned them.

Remembering her, he recalled the flash of her eyes, the proud lift of her chin, the way she walked.

He stared grimly into the night and swore softly. Was he in love? "Who knows?" he demanded viciously of the night. "And what good would it do if I was?"

He had never seen the Fort, yet knew it lay between the forks of the Piney and its approximate location. His way led across the billowing hills through a country marked by small streams lined with cottonwood, box elder, willow, choke-cherry and wild plum. That this was Indian country, he knew. The unrest of the tribes was about to break into open warfare. Already there had been sporadic attacks on haying or wood-cutting parties. Constant attacks were being made on the Missouri steamboats, far to the north.

Red Cloud, most influential chieftain among the Sioux, had tried to hold the tribes together, and despite the continued betrayal of treaties by the white man, had sought to abide by the code laid down for his. With Man Afraid Of His Hoss, the Ogallala chief, Red Cloud was the strongest of all the Sioux leaders.

With Custer's march into the Black Hills and the increasing travel over the Laramie and Bozeman trails, the Sioux were growing restless. The Sioux medicine man, Sitting Bull, was indulging in war talk, aided and abetted by two powerful warriors, skilled tacticians and great leaders, Crazy Horse and Gall.

No one in the West but understood that an outbreak of serious nature was overdue.

Rafe Caradec was aware of all this. He was aware, too, that it would not be an easy thing to prevail upon the doctor to leave the Fort, or upon the commandant to allow him to leave. In the face of impending trouble, his place was with the Army.

News of the battle of the Crazy Woman, after Ann's warning, reached her that evening. The return of the triumphant Shute riders was enough to tell her what had happened. She heard them ride into the street, heard their yells, and their shouts.

She heard that Bo Marsh was definitely dead. Even some of the Shute riders were harsh in their criticism of Tom Blazer for that action.

While the Shute outfit had ridden away following their attack, fearful of the effects of sharpshooting from the timber, they were satisfied. Winter was coming on, and they had destroyed the cabin on the Crazy Woman. Mistakenly, they also believed they had killed Brisco and wounded at least one other man.

Sick at heart, Ann had walked back into her room and stood by the window. Suddenly she was overwhelmed by the desire to get away, to escape all this sickening violence, the guns, the killings, the problems of frontier life. Back East there were lovely homes along quiet streets, slow-running streams, men who walked quietly on Sunday mornings. There were parties, theatres, friends, homes.

Her long ride had tired her. The touch of Rafe Caradec's hand, the look in his eyes had given her a lift. Something had sparked within her, and she felt herself drawn to him, yearning toward him with everything feminine that was within her. Riding away, she had heard the crash of guns, shouts and yells. Had she been too late?

Where was her sympathy? With Shute's riders? Or with this strange, tall young man who had come to claim half her ranch and tell fantastic stories of knowing her father aboard a ship?

Every iota of intelligence she had told her the man was all wrong, that his story could not be true. Bruce Barkow's story of her father's death had been the true one.

What reason for him to lie? Why would he want to claim her land when there was so much more to be had for the taking?

Her father had told her, and Gene Baker had agreed, that soon all this country would be open to settlement. There would be towns and railroads here. Why choose one piece of land, a large section of it worthless, when the hills lay bare for the taking?

Standing by the window and looking out into the darkness, Ann knew suddenly she was sick of it all. She would get away, go back East. Bruce was right. It was time she left here, and when he came again, she would tell him she was ready. He had been thoughtful and considerate. He had protected her, been attentive and affectionate. He was a man of intelligence, he was handsome. She could be proud of him.

She stifled her misgivings with a sudden resolution and hurriedly began to pack.

Vaguely Ann had sensed Barkow's fear of something, but she believed it was fear of an attack by Indians. Word had come earlier that day that the Ogallala were gathering in the hills and there was much war talk among them. That it could be Dan Shute whom Barkow feared, Ann had no idea.

She had completed the packing of the few items she would need for the trip when she heard the sound of gunfire from the National. The shots brought her to her feet with a start, her face pale. Running into the living room, she found that Gene Baker had caught up his rifle. She ran to Mrs. Baker and the two women stood together, listening.

Baker looked at them. "Can't be Indians," he said, after a moment. "Mebbe some wild cowhand celebratin'."

They heard excited voices, yells. Baker went to the door, hesitated, then went out. He was gone several minutes before he returned. His face was grave.

"It was that Texas rider from the Crazy Woman," he said. "He stepped into the back door of the National and shot it out with Tom Blazer and Fats McCabe. They are both dead."

"Was he alone?" Ann asked quickly.

Baker nodded, looking at her somberly. "They are huntin' him now. He won't get away, I'm afeerd."

"You're *afraid* he won't?"

"Yes, Ann," Baker said, "I am. That Blazer outfit's poison. All of that Shute bunch, far's that goes. Tom killed young Bo Marsh by stickin' a pistol against him whilst he was lyin' down."

The flat bark of a shot cut across the night air, and they went rigid. Two more shots rang out."

"Guess they got him," Baker said. "There's so many of them, I figgered they would."

Before the news reached them of what had actually happened, daylight had come. Ann Rodney was awake after an almost sleepless night. Tex Brisco, she heard, had killed Joe Gorman when Gorman had caught him at his horse. Tex had escaped, but from all the evidence, he was badly wounded. They were trailing him by the blood from his wounds.

Bo Marsh, now Brisco. Was Johnny Gill alive? Was Rafe? If Rafe was alive, then he must be alone, harried like a rabbit by hounds.

Restless, Ann paced the floor. Shute riders came into the store. They were buying supplies and going out in groups of four and five, scouring the hills for Brisco or any of the others of the Crazy Woman crowd.

Bruce Barkow came shortly after breakfast. He looked tired, worried. "Ann," he said abruptly, "if we're goin', it'll have to be today. This country is goin' to the wolves. All they think about now is killin'. Let's get out."

She hesitated only an instant. Something inside her seemed lost and dead.

"All right, Bruce. We've planned it for a long time. It might as well be now."

There was no fire in her, no spark. Barkow scarcely heeded that. She would go. Once away from here and married, he would have title to the land. Dan Shute, for all his talk and harsh ways, would be helpless.

"All right," he said. "We'll leave in an hour. Don't tell anybody. We'll take the buckboard like we were goin' for a drive, as we often do."

She was ready, so there was nothing to do after he had gone.

Baker seemed older, worried. Twice riders came in, and each time Ann heard that Tex Brisco was still at large. His horse had been trailed, seemingly wandering without guidance, to a place on a mountain creek. There the horse had walked into the water, and no trail had been found to show where he had left it. He was apparently headed for the high ridges, south by west.

Nor had anything been found of Marsh or Gill. Shute riders had returned to the Crazy Woman, torn down the corral, and hunted through the woods, but no sign had been found beyond a crude lean-to where the wounded man had evidently been sheltered. Marsh, if dead, had been buried and the grave concealed. Nothing had been found of any of them, although one horse had ridden off to the northeast, mostly east.

One horse had gone east! Ann Rodney's heart gave a queer leap. East would mean toward the Fort! Perhaps—but she was being foolish. Why should it be

Caradec rather than Gill, and why to the Fort? She expressed the thought, and Baker looked at her.

"Likely enough one of 'em's gone there. If Marsh ain't dead, and the riders didn't find his body, chances are he's mighty bad off. The only doctor around is at the Fort."

The door to the store opened, and Baker went in, leaving the living room. There was a brief altercation, then the curtain was pushed aside and Ann looked up. A start of fear went through her.

Dan Shute was standing in the door. For a wonder, he was clean-shaven except for his mustache. He looked at her with his queer, gray-white eyes.

"Don't you do nothin' foolish," he said, "like tryin' to leave here. I don't aim to let you."

Ann got up, amazed and angry. "You don't aim to let me?" she flared. "What business is it of yours?"

Shute stood there with his big hands on his hips staring at her insolently. "Because I want to make it my business," he said. "I've told Barkow where he stands with you. If he don't like it, he can say so and die. I ain't particular. I just wanted you should know that from here on you're my woman."

"Listen here, Shute!" Baker flared. "You can't talk to a decent woman that way!"

"Shut your mouth!" Shute said, staring at Baker. "I talk the way I please. I'm tellin' her. If she tries to get away from here, I'll take her out to the ranch now. If she waits"—he looked her up and down coolly—"I may marry her. Don't know why I should." He added, glaring at Baker, "You butt into this and I'll smash you. She ain't no woman for a weak sister like Barkow. I guess she'll come to like me all right. Anyway, she'd better." He turned toward the door. "Don't get any ideas. I'm the law here—the *only* law."

"I'll appeal to the Army!" Baker declared.

"You do," Shute said, "and I'll kill you. Anyway, the Army's goin' to be some busy. A bunch of Sioux raided a stage station way south of here last night and killed three men, then ran off the stock. Two men were killed hayin' over on Otter last night. A bunch of soldiers hayin' not far from the Piney were fired on and one man wounded. The Army's too busy to bother with the likes of you. Besides," he added, grinning, "the commandin' officer said that in case of Injun trouble, I was to take command at Painted Rock and make all preparations for defense."

He turned and walked out of the room. They heard the front door slam, and Ann sat down, suddenly.

Gene Baker walked to the desk and got out his gun. His face was stiff and old.

"No, not that," Ann said. "I'm leaving, Uncle Gene."

"Leavin'? How?" He turned on her, his eyes alert.

"With Bruce. He's asked me several times. I was going to tell you, but nobody else. I'm all packed."

"Barkow, eh?" Gene Baker stared at her. "Well, why not? He's half a gentleman, anyway. Shute is an animal and a brute."

The back door opened gently. Bruce Barkow stepped in.

"Was Dan here?"

Baker explained quickly. "Better forget that buckboard idea," he said, when Barkow had explained the plan. "Take the horses and go by the river trail. Leave at noon when everybody will be eatin'. Take the Bannock Trail, then swing north and east and cut around toward the Fort. They'll think you're tryin' for the gold fields."

Barkow nodded. He looked stiff and pale, and he was wearing a gun.

It was almost noon.

When the streets were empty, Bruce Barkow went out back to the barn and saddled the horses. There was no one in sight. The woods along the creek were only a hundred yards away.

Walking outside, the two got into their saddles and

rode at a walk, the dust muffling the beat of horse's hoofs, to the trees. Then they took the Bannock Trail. Two miles out, Barkow rode into a stream, then led the way north.

Once away from the trail they rode swiftly, keeping the horses at a rapid trot. Barkow was silent. His eyes kept straying to the back trail. Twice they saw Indian sign, but their escape had evidently been made successfully, for there was no immediate sound of pursuit.

Bruce Barkow kept moving. As he rode, his irritation, doubt, and fear began to grow more and more obvious. He rode like a man in the grip of deadly terror. Ann, watching him, wondered.

Before, Shute had tolerated Barkow. Now a definite break had been made, and with each mile of their escape, Barkow became more frightened. There was no way back now. He would be killed on sight, for Dan Shute was not a man to forgive or tolerate such a thing.

It was only on the girl's insistence that he stopped for a rest, and to give the horses a much needed blow. They took it, while Ann sat on the grass, and Bruce paced the ground, his eyes searching the trail over which they had come. When they were in the saddle again, he seemed to relax, to come to himself. Then he looked at her.

"You might think I'm a coward," he said, "but it's just that I'm afraid what Shute would do if he got his hands on you. I'm no gunfighter. He'd kill us both."

"I know." She nodded gravely.

This man who was to be her husband impressed her less at every moment. Somehow his claim that he was thinking of her failed to ring with sincerity. Yet with all his faults, he was probably only a weak man, a man cut out for civilization and not for the frontier.

They rode on, and the miles piled up behind them.

XII

RAFE CARADEC awakened with a start to the sound of a bugle. It took him several seconds to realize that he was in bed at the Fort. Then he remembered. The commanding officer had refused to allow the surgeon to leave before morning, and then only with an escort. With Lieutenant Ryson and eight men they would form a scouting patrol, would circle around by Crazy Woman, then cut back toward the Fort.

The party at the Fort was small, for the place had been abandoned several years before, and had been utilized only for a few weeks as a base for scouting parties when fear of an Indian outbreak began to grow. It was no longer an established post, but merely a camp.

Further to the south there was a post at Fort Fetterman, named for the leader of the troops trapped in the Fetterman Massacre. A wagon train had been attacked within a short distance of Fort Phil Kearney and a group of seventy-nine soldiers and two civilians were to march out to relieve them under command of Major James Powell, a skilled-Indian fighter. However, Brevet Lieutenant Colonel Fetterman had used his rank to take over the command, and had ridden out. Holding the fighting ability of the Indians in contempt, Fetterman had pursued some of them beyond a ridge. Firing had been heard. When other troops were sent out from the Fort they discovered Fetterman and his entire command wiped out, about halfway down the ridge. The wagon train they had gone to relieve reached the Fort later, unaware of the encounter.

Getting into his clothes, Rafe hurried outside. The first person he met was Ryson.

"Good morning, Caradec!" Ryson said, grinning. "Bugle wake you up?"

Caradec nodded. "It isn't the first time."

"You've been in the service then?" Ryson asked, glancing at him quickly.

"Yes." Rafe glanced around the stockade. "I was with Sully. In Mexico for a while, too, and Guatemala."

Ryson glanced at him. "Then you're *that* Caradec? Man, I've heard of you! Major Skehan will be pleased to know. He's an admirer of yours, sir!"

He nodded toward two weary, dust-covered horses.

"You're not the only arrival from Painted Rock," Ryson said. "Those horses came in last night. Almost daylight, in fact, with two riders. A chap named Barkow and a girl. Pretty, too, the lucky dog!"

Rafe turned on him, his eyes sharp. "A woman? A girl?"

Ryson looked surprised. "Why, yes. Her name's Rodney. She—"

"Where is she?" Rafe snapped. "Where is she now?"

Ryson smiled slightly. "Why, that's her over there! A friend of yours?"

But Rafe was gone.

Ann was standing in the door of one of the partly reconstructed buildings. When she saw him her eyes widened.

"Rafe! You here? Then you got away?"

"I came after a doctor for Marsh. He's in a bad way." He tossed the remark aside, studying her face. "Ann, what are you doing here with Barkow?"

His tone nettled her. "Why? How does it concern you?"

"Your father asked me to take care of you," he said,

"and if you married Bruce Barkow, I certainly wouldn't be doin' it!"

"Oh?" Her voice was icy. "Still claiming you knew my father? Well, Mr. Caradec, I think you'd be much better off to forget that story. I don't know where you got the idea, or how, or what made you believe you could get away with it, but it won't do! I've been engaged to Bruce for months. I intend to marry him now. There's a chaplain here. Then we'll go on to the river and down to St. Louis. There's a steamer on the way up that we can meet."

"I won't let you do it, Ann," Rafe said harshly.

Her weariness, her irritation, and something else brought quick anger to her face and lips.

"You won't *let* me? You have nothing to do with it! It simply isn't any of your business! Now, if you please, I'm waiting for Bruce. Will you go?"

"No," he said violently. "I won't! I'll say again what I said before. I knew your father. He gave me a deed givin' us the ranch. He asked me to care for you. He also gave me the receipt that Bruce Barkow gave him for the mortgage money. I wanted things to be different, Ann. I—"

"Caradec!" Ryson called. "We're ready!"

He glanced around. The small column awaited him, and his horse was ready. For an instant he glanced back at the girl. Her jaw was set, her eyes blazing.

"Oh, what's the use?" he flared. "Marry who you blasted well please!"

Wheeling, he walked to his horse and swung into the saddle, riding away without a backward glance.

Lips parted to speak, Ann Rodney stared after the disappearing riders. Suddenly all her anger was gone. She found herself gazing at the closing gate of the stockade and fighting a mounting sense of panic.

What had she done? Suppose what Rafe had said

was the truth? What had he ever done to make her doubt him?

Confused, puzzled by her own feelings for this stranger of whom she knew so little, yet who stirred her so deeply, she was standing there, one hand partly upraised when she saw two men come around the corner of the building. Both wore the rough clothing of miners.

They paused near her, one a stocky, thick-set man with a broad, hard jaw, the other a slender, blond young man.

"Ma'am," the younger man said, "we just come in from the river. The Major was tellin' us you were goin' back that way?"

She nodded dumbly, then forced herself to speak. "Yes, we are going to the river with some of the troops."

"We come up the Powder from the Yellowstone, ma'am," the younger man said, "and if you could tell us where to find your husband, we might sell him our boats."

She shook her head. "I'm not married yet. You will have to see my fiancé, Bruce Barkow. He's in the mess hall."

The fellow hesitated, turning his hat in his hand. "Ma'am, they said you was from Painted Rock. Ever hear tell of a man named Rafe Caradec over there?"

She stiffened. "Rafe Caradec?" She looked at him quickly. "You know him?"

He nodded, pleased by her sudden interest. "Yes, ma'am. We were shipmates of his. Me and my partner over there, Rock Mullaney. My name is Penn, ma'am, Roy Penn."

Suddenly her heart was pounding. She looked at him and bit her under lip. Then she said, carefully, "You were on a *ship* with him?"

"That's right."

Penn was puzzled and growing wary. After all, there was the manner of their leaving. Of course, that was months ago, and they were far from the sea now, but that still hung over them.

"Was there—aboard that ship—a man named Rodney?"

Ann couldn't look at them now. She stared at the stockade, almost afraid to hear their reply. Vaguely, she realized that Bruce Barkow was approaching.

"Rodney? Shorest thing you know! Charles Rodney. Nice feller, too. He died off the California coast after—" He hesitated. "Ma'am, you ain't no relation of his now?"

"I'm Charles Rodney's daughter."

"Oh?" Then Penn's eyes brightened. "Say, then you're the girl Rafe was lookin' for when he come over here! Think of that!" He turned. "Hey, Rock! This here's that Ann Rodney, the girl Rafe came here to see! You know, Charlie's daughter!"

Bruce Barkow stopped dead still. His dark face was suddenly wary. "What was that?" he said sharply. "What did you say?"

Penn stared at him. "No reason to get excited, mister. Yeah, we knew this young lady's father 'board ship. He was shanghaied out of San Francisco!"

Bruce Barkow's face was cold. Here it was at the last minute. This did it. He was trapped now. He could see in Ann's face the growing realization of how he had lied, how he had betrayed her, and even—he could see that coming into her eyes too—the idea that he had killed her father.

Veins swelled in his forehead and throat. He glared at Penn, half crouching, like some cornered animal. "You're a liar!" he snarled.

"Don't call me that!" Penn said fiercely. "I'm not wearing a gun, mister!"

If Barkow heard the last words they made no impression. His hand was already sweeping down. Penn stepped back, throwing his arms wide, and Bruce Barkow, his face livid with the fury of frustration, whipped

121

up a gun and shot him twice through the body. Penn staggered back, uncomprehending, staring.

"No—gun!" he gasped. "I don't—gun."

He staggered into an Army wagon, reeled, and fell headlong.

Bruce Barkow stared at the fallen man, then his contorted face turned upward. On the verge of escape and success he had been trapped, and now he had become a killer!

Wheeling, he sprang into the saddle. The gate was open for a wood wagon, and he whipped the horse through it, shouting hoarsely. Men had rushed from everywhere. Rock Mullaney, staring in shocked surprise, could only fumble at his belt. He wore no gun either.

He looked up at Ann. "We carried rifles," he muttered. "We never figgered on no trouble!" Then he rubbed his face, sense returning to his eyes. "Ma'am, what did he shoot him for?"

She stared at him, humbled by the grief written on the man's hard, lonely face. "That man, Barkow, killed my father!" she said.

"No, ma'am. If you're Charlie Rodney's daughter, Charlie died aboard ship with us."

She nodded. "I know, but Barkow was responsible. Oh, I've been a fool! An awful fool!"

An officer was kneeling over Penn's body. He got up, glanced at Mullaney, then at Ann.

"This man is dead," he said.

Resolution came suddenly to Ann. "Major," she said, "I'm going to catch that patrol. Will you lend me a fresh horse? Ours will still be badly worn-out after last night."

"It wouldn't be safe, Miss Rodney," he protested. "It wouldn't at all. There's Indians out there. How Caradec got through, or you and Barkow, is beyond me." He gestured to the body. "What do you know about this?"

Briefly, concisely, she explained, telling all. She made no attempt to spare herself or to leave anything out.

She outlined the entire affair, taking only a few minutes.

"I see." He looked thoughtfully at the gate. "If I could give you an escort, I would, but—"

"If she knows the way," Mullaney said, "I'll go with her. We came down the river from Fort Benton, then up the Yellowstone and the Powder. We thought we would come and see how Rafe was gettin' along. If we'd knowed there was trouble, we'd have come before."

"It's as much as your life is worth, man," the major warned.

Mullaney shrugged. "Like as not, but my life has had chances taken with it before. Besides"—he ran his fingers over his bald head—"there's no scalp here to attract Injuns!"

Well-mounted, Ann and Mullaney rode swiftly. The patrol would be hurrying because of Bo Marsh's serious condition, but they should overtake them, and following was no immediate problem.

Mullaney knew the West and had fought before in his life as a wandering jack-of-all-trades. He was not upset by the chance they were taking. He glanced from time to time at Ann, then rambling along, he began to give her an account of their life aboard ship, of the friendship that had grown between her father and Rafe Caradec, and all Rafe had done to spare the older man work and trouble.

He told her how Rafe had treated Rodney's wounds when he had been beaten, how he saved food for him, and how close the two had grown. Twice, noting her grief and shame, he ceased talking, but each time she insisted on his continuing.

"Caradec?" Mullaney said finally. "Well, I'd say he was one of the finest men I've known. A fighter, he is! The lad's a fighter from way back! You should have seen the beatin' he gave that Borger! I got only a glimpse, but Penn told me about it. And if it hadn't been for Rafe none of us would have got away. He planned it, and he carried it out. He planned it before your father's last trouble—the trouble that killed him—but when he saw your father would die, he carried on with it."

They rode on in silence. All the time, Ann knew now, she should have trusted her instincts. Always they had warned her about Bruce Barkow, always they had been sure of Rafe Caradec. As she sat in the jury box and watched him talk, handling his case, it had been his sincerity that impressed her, even more than his shrewd handling of questions.

He had killed men, yes. But what men! Bonaro and Trigger Boyne, both acknowledged and boastful killers of men themselves. Men unfit to walk in the tracks of such as Rafe. She had to find him! She must!

The wind was chill, and she glanced at Mullaney.

"It's cold," she said. "It feels like snow!"

He nodded grimly. "It does that!" he said. "Early for it, but it's happened before. If we get a norther now—" He shook his head.

They made camp while it was still light. Mullaney built a fire of dry sticks that gave off almost no smoke. Water was heated, and they made coffee. While Ann was fixing the little food they had, he rubbed the horses down with handfuls of dry grass.

"Can you find your way in the dark?" he asked her.

"Yes, I think so. It is fairly easy from here, for we have the mountains. That highest peak will serve as a landmark unless there are too many clouds."

"All right," he said, "we'll keep movin'."

She found herself liking the burly seaman and cowhand. He helped her smother the fire and wipe out traces of it.

"If we can stick to the trail of the soldiers," he said, "it'll confuse the Injuns. They'll think we're with their party."

They started on. Ann led off, keeping the horses at

a fast walk. Night fell, and with it, the wind grew stronger. After an hour of travel, Ann reined in.

Mullaney rode up beside her. "What's the matter?"

She indicated the tracks of a single horse crossing the route of the soldiers.

"You think it's this Barkow?" He nodded as an idea came. "It could be. The soldiers don't know what happened back there. He might ride with 'em for protection."

Another thought came to him. He looked at Ann keenly. "Suppose he'd try to kill Caradec?"

Her mind jumped. "Oh, no!" She was saying no to the thought, not to the possibility. She knew it was a possibility. What did Bruce have to lose? He was already a fugitive, and another killing would make it no worse. And Rafe Caradec had been the cause of it all.

"He might," she agreed. "He might, at that."

Miles to the west, Bruce Barkow, his rifle across his saddle, leaned into the wind. He had followed the soldiers for a way, and the idea of a snipe shot at Caradec stayed in his mind. He could do it, and they would think the Indians had done it.

But there was a better way. A way to get at them all. If he could ride on ahead, reach Gill and Marsh before the patrol did, he might kill them, then get Caradec when he approached. If then he could get rid of Shute, Gomer would have to swing with him to save something from the mess. Maybe Dan Shute's idea was right, after all! Maybe killing was the solution.

Absorbed by the possibilities of the idea, Barkow turned off the route followed by the soldiers. There was a way that could make it safer and somewhat faster. He headed for the old Bozeman Trail, now abandoned.

He gathered his coat around him to protect him from the increasing cold. His mind was fevered with worry, doubt of himself, and mingled with it was hatred of

Caradec, Shute, Ann Rodney, and everything. He drove on into the night.

Twice, he stopped to rest. The second time he started on, it was turning gray with morning. As he swung into saddle, a snowflake touched his cheek.

He thought little of it. His horse was uneasy, though, and anxious for the trail. Snow was not a new thing, and Barkow scarcely noticed as the flakes began to come down thicker and faster.

Gill and the wounded man had disappeared, he knew. Shute's searchers had not found them near the house. Bruce Barkow had visited that house many times before the coming of Caradec, and he knew the surrounding hills well. About a half mile back from the house, sheltered by a thick growth of lodgepole, was a deep cave among some rocks. If Johnny Gill had found that cave, he might have moved Marsh there.

It was, at least, a chance.

Bruce Barkow was not worried about the tracks he was leaving. Few Indians would be moving in this inclement weather. Nor would the party from the Fort have come this far north. From the route they had taken he knew they were keeping to the low country.

He was nearing the first range of foothills now, the hills that divided Long Valley from the open plain that sloped gradually away to the Powder and the old Bozeman Trail. He rode into the pines and started up the trail, intent upon death. His mind was sharpened like that of a hungry coyote. Cornered and defeated for the prize himself, his only way out, either for victory or revenge, lay in massacre. Wholesale killing.

It was like him that having killed once, he did not hesitate to accept the idea of killing again.

He did not see the big man on the gray horse who fell in behind him. He did not glance back over his trail, although by now the thickening snow obscured the background so much that the rider, gaining slowly on him through the storm, would have been no more than a shadow.

To the right, behind the once bald and now snow-covered dome, was the black smear of seeping oil. Drawing abreast of it, Bruce Barkow reined in and glanced down.

Here it was, the cause of it all. The key to wealth, to everything a man could want. Men had killed for less, he could kill for this. He knew where there were four other such seepages and the oil sold from twenty dollars to thirty dollars the barrel.

He got down and stirred it with a stick. It was thick now, thickened by cold. Well, he still might win.

Then he heard a shuffle of footsteps in the snow, and looked up. Dan Shute's figure was gigantic in the heavy coat he wore, sitting astride the big horse. He looked down at Barkow, and his lips parted.

"Tried to get away with her, did you? I knew you had coyote in you, Barkow."

His hand came up, and in the gloved hand was a pistol. In a sort of shocked disbelief, Bruce Barkow saw the gun lift. His own gun was under his short, thick coat.

"No!" he gasped hoarsely. "Not that! *Dan!*"

The last word was a scream, cut sharply off by the sharp, hard bark of the gun. Bruce Barkow folded slowly and, clutching his stomach, toppled across the black seepage, staining it with a slow shading of red.

For a minute Dan Shute sat his horse, staring down. Then he turned the horse and moved on. He had an idea of his own. Before the storm began, from a mountain ridge he picked out the moving patrol. Behind it were two figures. He had a hunch about those two riders, striving to overtake the patrol.

He would see.

XIII

PUSHING RAPIDLY AHEAD through the falling snow the patrol came up to the ruins of the cabin on the Crazy Woman on the morning of the second day out from the Fort. Steam rose from the horses, and the breath of horses and men fogged the air.

There was no sign of life. Rafe swung down and stared about. The smooth surface of the snow was unbroken, yet he could see that much had happened since he started his trek to the Fort for help. The lean-to, not quite complete, was abandoned.

Lieutenant Ryson surveyed the scene thoughtfully.

"Are we too late?" he asked.

Caradec hesitated, staring around. There was no hope in what he saw. "I don't think so," he said. "Johnny Gill was a smart hand. He would figger out somethin'. Besides, I don't see any bodies."

In his mind, he surveyed the canyon. Certainly Gill could not have gone far with the wounded man. Also, it would have to be in the direction of possible shelter. The grove of lodgepoles offered the best chance. Turning, he walked toward them. Ryson dismounted his men, and they started fires.

Milton Waitt, the surgeon, stared after Rafe, then walked in his tracks. When he came up with him, he suggested:

"Any caves around?"

Caradec paused, considering that. "There may be. None that I know of, though. Still, Johnny prowled in these rocks a lot and may have found one. Let's have a look." Then a thought occurred to him. "They'd have to have water, Doc. Let's go to the spring."

There was ice over it, but the ice had been broken and had frozen again. Rafe indicated it. "Somebody drank here since the cold set in."

He knelt and felt of the snow with his fingers, working his way slowly around the spring. Suddenly he stopped.

"Found something?" Waitt watched curiously. This made no sense to him.

"Yes, whoever got water from the spring splashed some on this side. It froze. I can feel the ice it made. That's a fair indication that whoever got water came from that side of the spring."

Moving around, he kept feeling of the snow.

"Here." He felt again. "There's an icy ring where he set the bucket for a minute. Water left on the bottom froze." He straightened, studying the mountainside. "He's up there, somewhere. He's got a bucket and he's able to come down here for water, but findin' him'll be the devil's own job. He'll need fuel, though. Somewhere he's been breakin' sticks and collectin' wood, but wherever he does it won't be close to his shelter. Gill's too smart for that."

Studying the hillside, Rafe indicated the nearest clump of trees.

"He wouldn't want to be out in the open on this snow any longer than he had to," he said thoughtfully, "and the chances are he'd head for the shelter of those trees. When he got there, he would probably set the bucket down while he studied the back trail and made sure he hadn't been seen."

Waitt nodded, his interest aroused. "Good reasoning, man. Let's see."

They walked to the clump of trees. After a few

minutes of search, Waitt found the same icy frozen place just under the thin skimming of snow.

"Where do we go from here?" he asked.

Rafe hesitated, studying the trees. A man would automatically follow the line of easiest travel, and there was an opening between the trees. He started on, then stopped.

"This is right. See? There's not so much snow on this branch. There's a good chance he brushed it off in passin'."

It was mostly guesswork, he knew. Yet after they had gone three hundred yards Rafe looked up and saw the cliff pushing its rocky shoulder in among the trees. At its base was a tumbled cluster of gigantic boulders and broken slabs.

He led off for the rocks. Almost the first thing he saw was a fragment of loose bark lying on the snow, and a few crumbs of dust such as is sometimes found between the bark and tree. He pointed it out to Waitt.

"He carried wood this way."

They paused there, and Rafe sniffed the air. There was no smell of woodsmoke. Were they dead? Had cold done what rifle bullets couldn't do? No, he decided, Johnny Gill knew too well how to take care of himself.

Rafe walked between the rocks, turning where it felt natural to turn. Suddenly, he saw a tipped-up slab of granite leaning against a larger boulder. It looked dry underneath. He stooped and glanced in. It was dark and silent, yet some instinct seemed to tell him it was not so empty as it appeared.

He crouched in the opening, leaving light from outside to come in first along one wall, then another. His keen eyes picked out a damp spot on the leaves. There was no place for a leak, and the wind had been in the wrong direction to blow in here.

"Snow," he said. "Probably fell off a boot."

They moved into the cave, bending over to walk.

Yet it was not really a cave at first, merely a slab of rock offering partial shelter.

About fifteen feet further along the slab ended under a thick growth of pine boughs and brush that formed a canopy overhead which offered almost as solid shelter as the stone itself. Then, on the rock face of the cliff, they saw a cave, a place gouged by wind and water long since, and completely obscured behind the boulders and brush from any view but where they stood.

They walked up to the entrance. The overhang of the cliff offered a shelter that was all of fifty feet deep, running along one wall of a diagonal gash in the cliff that was invisible from outside. They stepped in on the dry sand, and had taken only a step when they smelled woodsmoke. At almost the same instant, Johnny Gill spoke.

"Hi, Rafe!" He stepped down from behind a heap of debris against one wall of the rock fissure. "I couldn't see who you were till now. I had my rifle ready so's if you were the wrong one I could discourage you." His face looked drawn and tired. "He's over here, Doc," Gill continued, "and he's been delirious all night."

While Waitt was busy over the wounded man, Gill walked back up the cave with Rafe.

"What's happened," Gill asked. "I thought they'd got you."

"No, they haven't, but I don't know much of what's been goin' on. Ann's at the Fort with Barkow, says she's goin' to marry him."

"What about Tex?" Gill asked quickly.

Rafe shook his head, scowling. "No sign of him. I don't know what's come off at Painted Rock. I'm leavin' for there as soon as I've told the lieutenant and his patrol where Doc is. You'll have to stick here because the Doc has to get back to the Fort."

"You goin' to Painted Rock?"

"Yes, I'm goin' to kill Dan Shute

"I'd like to see that," Gill said grimly, "but watch

yourself!" The little cowhand looked at him seriously. "Boss, what about that girl?"

Rafe's lips tightened and he stared at the bare wall of the cave.

"I don't know," he said grimly. "I tried to talk her out of it, but I guess I wasn't what you'd call tactful."

Gill stuck his thumbs in his belt. "Tell her you're in love with her yourself?"

Caradec stared at him. "Where'd you get that idea?"

"Readin' sign. You ain't been the same since you ran into her the first time. She's your kind of people, Boss."

"Mebbe. But looks like she reckoned she wasn't. Never would listen to me give the straight story on her father. Both of us flew off the handle this time."

"Well, I ain't no hand at ridin' herd on womenfolks, but I've seen a thing or two, Boss. The chances are if you'd 'a' told her you're in love with her, she'd never have gone with Bruce Barkow."

Rafe was remembering those words when he rode down the trail toward Painted Rock. What lay ahead of him could not be planned. He had no idea when or where he would encounter Dan Shute. He knew only that he must find him.

After reporting to Ryson, Rafe had hit the trail for Painted Rock alone. By now he knew that mountain trail well. Even the steady fall of snow failed to make him change his mind about making the ride.

He was burning up inside. The old, driving recklessness was in him, the urge to be in and shooting. His enemies were in the clear, and all the cards were on the table in plain sight.

Barkow, he discounted. Dan Shute was the man to get, and Pod Gomer, the man to watch. What he intended to do was high-handed, as high-handed in its way as what Shute and Barkow had attempted, but in Rafe's case the cause was just.

132

Mullaney had stopped in a wooded draw short of the hills. He stopped for a short rest just before daybreak on that fatal second morning. The single rider had turned off from the trail and was no longer with the patrol. Both he and the girl needed rest, aside from the horses.

He kicked snow away from the grass, then swept some of it clear with a branch. In most places it was already much too thick for that. After he made coffee and they had eaten, he got up. "Get ready," he said, "and I'll get the horses."

All night he had been thinking of what he would do when he found Barkow. He had seen the man draw on Penn, and he was not fast. That made it an even break, for Mullaney knew that he was not fast himself.

When he found the horses missing, he stopped. Evidently they had pulled their picket pins and wandered off. He started on, keeping in their tracks. He did not see the big man in the heavy coat who stood in the brush and watched him.

Dan Shute threaded his way down to the campfire. When Ann looked up at his approach, she thought at first it was Mullaney, and then she recognized Shute.

Eyes wide, she came to her feet. "Why, hello! What are you doing here?"

He smiled at her, his eyes sleepy and yet wary. "Huntin' you. Reckoned this was you. When I seen Barkow I reckoned somethin' had gone wrong."

"You saw Bruce? Where?"

"North a ways. He won't bother you none." Shute smiled. "Barkow was spineless. Thought he was smart. He never was half as smart as that Caradec, nor as tough as me."

"What happened?" Ann's heart was pounding. Mullaney should be coming now. He would hear their voices and be warned.

"I killed him." Shute was grinning cynically. "He wasn't much good." Shute smiled. "Don't be wonderin'

133

about that hombre with you. I led his horses off and turned 'em adrift. He'll be hours catchin' 'em, if he ever does. However, he might come back, so we'd better drift."

"No," Ann said, "I'll wait."

He smiled again. "Better come quiet. If he came back, I'd have to kill him. You don't want him killed, do you?"

She hesitated only a moment. This man would stop at nothing. He was going to take her if he had to knock her out and tie her. Better anything than that. If she appeared to play along, she might have a chance.

"I'll go," she said simply. "You have a horse?"

"I kept yours," he said. "Mount up."

By the time Rafe Caradec was en route to Painted Rock, Dan Shute was riding with his prisoner into the ranchyard of his place near Painted Rock. Far to the south and west, Rock Mullaney long since had come up to the place where Shute had finally turned his horse loose and ridden on, leading the other. Mullaney kept on the trail of the lone horse and came up with it almost a mile further.

Lost and alone in the thickly falling snow, the animal hesitated at his call, then waited for him to catch up. When he was mounted once more he turned back to his camp, and the tracks, nearly covered, told him little. The girl, accompanied by another rider, had ridden away. She would never have gone willingly.

Mullaney was worried. During their travel they had talked little, yet Ann had supplied a few of the details. He knew vaguely about Dan Shute, about Bruce Barkow. He also knew than an Indian outbreak was feared.

Mullaney knew something about Indians, and doubted any trouble until spring or summer. There might be occasional shootings, but Indians were not, as a rule, cold weather fighters. For that he didn't blame them. Yet any wandering hunting or foraging parties must be avoided. It was probable that any warrior or group of them coming along a fresh trail would follow it and count coup on an enemy if possible.

He knew roughly the direction of Painted Rock, yet instinct told him he had better stick to the tangible and near, so he swung back to the trail of the Army patrol and headed for the pass into Long Valley.

Painted Rock lay still under the falling snow when Rafe Caradec drifted down the street on the big black. He swung down in front of the Emporium and went in.

Baker looked up, and his eyes grew alert when he saw Rafe's entrance. At Caradec's question, he told him of what had happened to Tex Brisco as far as he knew. He also told him of Dan Shute's arrival and threat to Ann, and her subsequent escape with Barkow. Baker was relieved to know they were at the Fort.

A wind was beginning to moan around the eaves, and they listened a minute. "Won't be good to be out in that," the storekeeper said gravely. "Sounds like a blizzard comin'. If Brisco's found shelter, he might be all right."

"Not in this cold," Caradec said, scowling. "No man with his resistance lowered by a wound is going to last in this. And it's going to be worse before it's better."

Standing there at the counter, letting the warmth of the big pot-bellied stove work through his system, Rafe assayed his position. Bo Marsh, while in bad shape, had been tended by a doctor and would have Gill's care. There was nothing more to be done there for the time being.

Ann had made her choice. She had gone off with Barkow. In his heart he knew that if there was any choice between Barkow or Shute she had made the better. Yet there had been another choice—or had there? Yes, she could at least have listened to him.

The Fort was far away, and all he could do now was trust to Ann's innate good sense to change her mind before it was too late. In any event, he could not get back there in time to do anything about it.

"Where's Shute?" he demanded.

"Ain't seen him," Baker said worriedly. "Ain't seen hide nor hair of him. But I can promise you one thing, Caradec. He won't take Barkow's runnin' out with Ann lyin' down. He'll be on their trail."

The door opened in a flurry of snow and Pat Higley pushed in. He pulled off his mittens and extended stiff fingers toward the red swell of the stove. He glanced at Rafe.

"Hear you askin' about Shute?" he asked. "I just seen him headed for the ranch. He wasn't alone, neither." He rubbed his fingers. "Looked to me like a woman ridin' along."

Rafe looked around. "A woman?" he asked carefully. "Now who would that be?"

"He's found Ann!" Baker exclaimed.

"She was at the Fort," Rafe said, "with Barkow. He couldn't take her away from the soldiers."

"No, he couldn't," Baker agreed, "but she might have left on her own. She's a stubborn girl when she takes a notion. After you left she may have changed her mind."

Rafe pushed the thought away. The chance was too slight. And where was Tex Brisco?

"Baker," he suggested, "you and Higley know this country. You know about Tex. Where do you reckon he'd wind up?"

Higley shrugged. "There's no tellin'. It ain't as if he knew the country, too. They trailed him for a while, and they said it looked like his hoss was wanderin' loose without no hand on the bridle. Then the hoss took to water, so Brisco must have come to his senses somewhat. Anyway, they lost his trail when he was ridin' west along a fork of Clear Creek. If he held to that direction it would take him over some plumb high, rough country south of the big peak. If he did get across, he'd wind up somewhere down along Tensleep Canyon, mebbe. But that's all guesswork."

"Any shelter that way?"

"Nary a mite, if you mean human shelter. There's plenty of timber there, but wolves, too. There's also plenty of shelter in the rocks. The only humans over that way are the Sioux, and they ain't in what you'd call a friendly mood. That's where Man Afraid Of His Hoss has been holed up."

Finding Tex Brisco would be like hunting a needle in a haystack, but it was what Rafe Caradec had to do. He had to make the effort. Yet the thought of Dan Shute and the girl returned to him. Suppose it was Ann? He shuddered to think of her in Shute's hands. The man was without a spark of decency or mercy.

"No use goin' out in this storm," Baker said. "You can stay with us, Caradec."

"You've changed your tune some, Baker," Rafe suggested grimly.

"A man can be wrong, can't he?" Baker inquired testily. "Mebbe I was. I don't know. Things have gone to perdition around here fast, ever since you came in here with that story about Rodney."

"Well, I'm not stayin'," Rafe told him. "I'm going to look for Tex Brisco."

The door was pushed open and they looked around. It was Pod Gomer. The sheriff looked even squarer and more bulky in a heavy buffalo coat. He cast a bleak look at Caradec, then walked to the fire, sliding out of his overcoat.

"You still here?" he asked, glancing at Rafe out of the corners of his eyes.

"Yes, I'm still here, Gomer, but you're traveling."

"What?"

"You heard me. You can wait till the storm is over, then get out, and keep movin'."

Gomer turned, his square hard face dark with angry blood.

"You—tellin' me?" he said furiously. "I'm sheriff here!"

"You were," Caradec said calmly. "Ever since you've been here you've been hand in glove with Barkow and Shute, runnin' their dirty errands for them, pickin' up the scraps they tossed you. Well, the fun's over. You slope out of here when the storm's over. Barkow's gone, and within a few hours Shute will be too."

"Shute?" Gomer was incredulous. "You'd go up against Dan Shute? Why, man, you're insane!"

"Am I?" Rafe shrugged. "That's neither here nor there. I'm talkin' to you. Get out and stay out. You can take your tinhorn judge with you."

Gomer laughed. "You're the one who's through! Marsh dead, Brisco either dead or on the dodge, and Gill mebbe dead. What chance have you got?"

"Gill's in as good shape as I am," Rafe said calmly, "and Bo Marsh is gettin' Army care, and he'll be out of the woods, too. As for Tex, he got away, and I'm bankin' on that Texan to come out walkin'. How much stomach are you boys goin' to have for the fight when Gill and I ride in here? Tom Blazer's gone, and so are a half-dozen more. Take your coat"—Rafe picked it up with his left hand—"and get out. If I see you after this storm, I'm shootin' on sight. Now, get!"

He heaved the heavy coat at Gomer, and the sheriff ducked, his face livid. Yet surprisingly he did not reach for a gun. He lunged and swung with his fist. A shorter man than Caradec, he was wider and thicker, a powerfully built man who was known in mining and trail camps as a rough-and-tumble fighter.

Caradec turned, catching Gomer's right on the cheekbone, but bringing up a solid punch to Gomer's midsection. The sheriff lunged close and tried to butt, and Rafe stabbed him in the face with a left, then smeared him with a hard right.

It was no match. Pod Gomer had fancied himself as a fighter, but Caradec had too much experience. He knocked Gomer back into a heap of sacks, then walked in on him and slugged him wickedly in the middle with both hands. Gomer went to his knees.

"All right, Pod," Rafe said, panting, "I told you. Get goin'."

The sheriff stayed on his knees, breathing heavily, blood dripping from his smashed nose. Rafe Caradec slipped into his coat and walked to the door.

Outside, he took the horse to the livery stable, brushed him off, then gave him a rub-down and some oats. He did not return to the store, but after a meal, saddled his horse and headed for Dan Shute's ranch. He couldn't escape the idea that the rider with Shute might have been Ann, despite the seeming impossibility of her being this far west. If she had left the Fort within a short time after the patrol, then it might be.

XIV

Dan Shute's ranch lay in a hollow-of the hills near a curving stream. Not far away the timber ran down to the plain's edge and dwindled away into a few scattered groves, blanketed now in snow.

A thin trail of smoke lifted from the chimney of the house, another from the bunkhouse. Rafe Caradec decided on boldness as the best course, and his muffled, snow-covered appearance to disguise him until within gun range. He opened a button on the front of his coat so he could get a gun thrust into his waist band.

He removed his right hand from its glove and thrust it deep in his pocket. There it would be warm and at the same time free to grasp the six-gun when he needed it.

No one showed. It was very cold. If there was anyone around who noticed his approach their curiosity did not extend to the point where they would come outside to investigate.

Rafe rode directly to the house, walked up on the porch, and rapped on the door with his left hand. There was no response. He rapped again, much harder.

All was silence. The mounting wind made hearing difficult, and he put his ear to the door and listened. There was no sound.

He dropped his left hand to the door and turned the knob. The door opened easily, and he let it swing wide, standing well out of line. The wind howled in, and a few flakes of snow, but there was no sound. He stepped inside and closed the door after him.

His ears tingled with cold, and he resisted a desire to rub them, then let his eyes sweep the wide room. A fire burned in the huge stone fireplace, but there was no one in the long room. Two exits from the room were hung with blankets. There was a table littered with odds and ends, and one end held some dirty dishes where a hasty meal had been eaten. Beneath that spot was a place showing dampness as though a pair of boots had shed melting snow.

There was no sound in the long room but the crackle of the fire and the low moan of the wind around the eaves. Walking warily, Rafe stepped over a saddle and some bits of harness and walked across to the opposite room. He pushed the blanket aside. Empty. An unmade bed of tumbled blankets, and a lamp standing on a table by the bed.

Rafe turned and stared at the other door, then looked back into the bedroom. There was a pair of dirty socks lying there and he stepped over and felt of them. They were damp.

Someone, within the last hour or less, had changed socks here. Walking outside he noticed something he had not seen before. Below a chair near the table was another spot of dampness. Apparently, two people had been here.

He stepped back into the shadow of the bedroom door and put his hand in the front of his coat. He hadn't wanted to reach for that gun in case anyone was watching. Now, with his hand on the gun, he stepped out of the bedroom and walked to the other blanket-covered door. He pushed it aside.

A large kitchen. A fire glowed in the huge sheet metal stove, and there was a coffee pot filled with boiling coffee. Seeing it, Rafe let go of his gun and picked up a cup. When he had filled it, he looked around the unkempt room. Like the rest of the house it was strongly built, but poorly kept inside. The floor was dirty with uncleaned dishes and scraps of food lying around.

He lifted the coffee cup, then his eyes saw a bit of white. He put down the cup and stepped over to the end of the woodpile. His heart jumped. It was a woman's handkerchief!

Quickly Rafe Caradec glanced around. Again he looked at the handkerchief in his hand and lifted it to his nostrils. There was a faint whiff of perfume, a scent he remembered only too well.

She had been here, then. The other rider with Dan Shute had been Ann Rodney. But where was she now? Where could she be? What had happened?

He gulped a mouthful of the hot coffee and stared around again. The handkerchief had been near the back door. He put down the coffee and eased the door open. Beyond was the barn and a corral. He walked outside. Pushing through the curtain of blowing snow, he reached the corral, then the barn.

Several horses were there. Hurrying along, he found two with dampness marking the places where their saddles had been. One of them he recalled as Ann's horse. He had seen the mount when he had been at the store.

There were no saddles showing any evidence of having been ridden, and the saddles would be sweaty underneath if they had been. Evidently, two horses had been saddled and ridden away from this barn.

Scowling, Rafe stared around. In the dust of the floor he found a small track, almost obliterated by a larger one. Had Shute saddled two horses and taken the girl away? If so, where would he take her and why? He decided suddenly that Shute had not taken Ann from here. She must have slipped away, saddled a horse, and escaped.

It was a far-fetched conclusion, but it offered not only

the solution he wanted, but one that fitted with the few facts available.

Why would Shute take the girl away from his ranch home? There was no logical reason. Especially in such a storm as this when as far as Shute knew there would be no pursuit? Rafe himself would not have done it. Perhaps Shute had been overconfident, believing Ann would rather share the warmth and security of the house than the mounting blizzard.

Only the bunkhouse remained unexplored. There was a chance they had gone there. Turning, Rafe walked to the bunkhouse. Shoving the door open, he stepped inside.

Four men sat on bunks. One, his boots off and his socks propper toward the stove, stared glumly at him from a chair made of a barrel.

The faces of all the men were familiar, but he could put a name to none of them. They had seen the right hand in the front of his coat, and they sat quietly, appreciating its significance.

"Where's Dan Shute?" he demanded, finally.

"Ain't seen him," said the man in the barrel chair.

"That go for all of you?" Rafe's eyes swung from one to the other.

A lean, hard-faced man with a scar on his jawbone grinned, showing yellow teeth. He raised himself on his elbow.

"Why, no. It shore don't, pilgrim. I seen him. He rode up here nigh on to an hour ago with that there girl from the store. They went inside. S'pose you want to get killed, you go to the house."

"I've been there. It's empty."

The lean-faced man sat up. "That right? That don't make sense. Why would a man with a filly like that take off into the storm?"

Rafe Caradec studied them coldly. "You men," he said, "had better sack up and get out of here when the storm's over. Dan Shute's through."

"Ain't you countin' unbranded stock, pardner?" the lean-faced man said, smiling tauntingly. "Dan Shute's able to handle his own troubles. He took care of Barkow."

This was news to Rafe. "He did? How'd you know that?"

"He done told me. Barkow run off with this girl and Shute trailed him. I didn't only see Shute come back, I talked some with him, and I unsaddled his hosses." He picked up a boot and pulled it on. "This here Rodney girl, she left the Fort, runnin' away from Barkow, and takin' after the Army patrol that rode out with you. Shute, he seen 'em. He also seen Barkow. He hunted Bruce down and shot him near that bare dome in your lower valley. When he left Barkow, he caught up with the girl and this strange hombre with her. Shute led their horses off, then got the girl while this hombre was huntin' them."

The explanation cleared up several points for Rafe. He stared thoughtfully around.

"You didn't see 'em leave here?"

"Not us," the lean-faced puncher said dryly. "None of us hired on for punchin' cows or ridin' herd on women in blizzards. Come a storm, we hole up and set her out. We aim to keep on doin' just that."

Rafe backed to the door and stepped out. The wind tore at his garments, and he backed away from the building. Within twenty feet it was lost behind a curtain of blowing snow. He stumbled back to the house.

More than ever, he was convinced that somehow Ann had escaped. Yet where to look? In this storm there was no direction, nothing. If she headed for town, she might make it. However, safety for her would more likely lie toward the mountains, for there she could improvise shelter, and probably last the storm out. Knowing the country, she would know how long such storms lasted. It was rarely more than three days.

He had little hope of finding Ann, yet he knew she

would never return here. Seated in the ranchhouse, he coolly ate a hasty meal and drank more coffee. Then he returned to his horse which he had led to the stable. Mounting, he rode out into the storm and on the way to town.

Gene Baker and Pat Higley looked up when Rafe Caradec came in. Baker's face paled when he saw that Rafe was alone.

"Did you find out?" he asked. "Was it Ann?"

Briefly, Rafe explained, telling all he had learned and his own speculations as to what had happened.

"She must have got away," Higley agreed. "Shute would never take her away from his ranch in this storm. But where could she have gone?"

Rafe explained his own theories on that. "She probably took it for granted he would think she would head for town," he suggested, "so she may have taken to the mountains. After all, she would know that Shute would kill anybody who tried to stop him."

Gene Baker nodded miserably. "That's right. What can a body do?"

"Wait," Higley said. "Just wait."

"I won't wait," Rafe said. "If she shows up here, hold her. Shoot Dan if you have to, drygulch him or anything. Get him out of the way. I'm goin' into the mountains. I can at least be lookin', and I might stumble onto some kind of a trail."

Two hours later, shivering with cold, Rafe Caradec acknowledged how foolhardy he had been. His black horse was walking steadily through a snow-covered avenue among the pines, weaving around fallen logs and clumps of brush. He had found nothing that resembled a trail, and twice he had crossed the stream. This, he knew, was also the direction that had been taken by the wounded Tex Brisco.

No track could last more than a minute in the whirling snow-filled world in which Rafe now rode. The wind howled and tore at his garments, even within the partial shelter of the lodgepoles. Yet he rode on, then dismounted and walked ahead, resting the horse. It was growing worse instead of better, yet he pushed on, taking the line of least resistance, sure that this was what the fleeing Ann would have done.

The icy wind ripped at his clothing, at times faced him like a solid, moving wall. The black stumbled wearily, and Rafe was suddenly contrite. The big horse had taken a brutal beating in these last few days. Even its great strength was weakening.

Squinting his eyes against the blowing snow, he stared ahead. He could see nothing, but he was aware that the wall of the mountain was on his left. Bearing in that direction, he came up to a thicker stand of trees and some scattered boulders. He rode on, alert for some possible shelter for himself and his horse.

Almost an hour later, he found it, a dry, sandy place under the overhang of the cliff, sheltered from the wind and protected from the snow by the overhang and by the trees and brush that fronted it. Swinging down, Rafe led the horse into the shelter and hastily built a fire.

From the underside of a log he got some bark, great sheets of it, and some fibrous, rotting wood. Then he broke some low branches on the trees, dead and dry. In a few minutes his fire was burning nicely. Then he stripped the saddle from the horse and rubbed him down with a handful of crushed bark. When that was done he got out the nosebag and fed the horse some of the oats he had appropriated from Shute's barn.

The next hour he occupied himself in gathering fuel. Luckily, there were a number of dead trees close by, debris left from some landslide from up the mountain. He settled down by the fire, made coffee. Dozing against the rock, he fed the blaze intermittently, his mind far away.

Somehow, sometime, he fell asleep. Around the rocks the wind, moaning and whining, sought with icy fingers for a grasp at his shoulder, at his hands. But the log burned well, and the big horse stood close, stamping in the sand and dozing beside the man on the ground.

Once, starting from his sleep, Rafe noticed that the log had burned until it was out of the fire, so he dragged it around, then laid another across it. Soon he was again asleep.

He awakened suddenly. It was daylight, and the storm was still raging. His fire blazed among the charred embers of his logs, and he lifted his eyes.

Six Indians faced him beyond the fire, and their rifles and bows covered him. Their faces were hard and unreadable. Two stepped forward and jerked him to his feet, stripped his guns from him and motioned for him to saddle his horse.

Numb with cold, he could scarcely realize what had happened to him. One of the Indians, wrapped in a worn red blanket, jabbered at the others and kept pointing to the horse making threatening gestures. Yet when Rafe had the animal saddled, they motioned to him to mount. Two of the Indians rode up then, leading the horses of the others.

So this was the way it ended. He was a prisoner.

XV

Uncomprehending, Rafe Caradec opened his eyes to darkness. He sat up abruptly and stared around. Then, after a long minute, it came to him. He was a prisoner in a village of the Ogallala Sioux, and he had just awakened.

Two days before they had brought him here, bound him hand and foot, and left him in the tepee he now occupied. Several times squaws had entered the tepee and departed. They had given him food and water.

It was night, and his wrists were swollen from the tightness of the bonds. It was warm in the tepee, for there was a fire, but smoke filed the skin wigwam and filtered but slowly out at the top. He had a feeling it was almost morning.

What had happened at Painted Rock? Where was Ann? And where was Tex Brisco? Had Dan Shute returned?

He was rolling over toward the entrance to catch a breath of fresh air whhen the flap was drawn back and a squaw came in. She caught him by the collar and dragged him back, but made no effort to molest him. He was more worried about the squaws than the braves, for they were given to torture.

Suddenly, the flap was drawn back again and two people came in, a warrior and a squaw. She spoke rapidly in Sioux, then picked a brand from the fire, and as it blazed up, held it close to his face. He drew back, thinking she meant to sear his eyes. Then, looking beyond the blaze, he saw that the squaw holding it was the Indian girl he had saved from Trigger Boyne!

With a burst of excited talk, she bent over him. A knife slid under his bonds and they were cut. Chafing his ankles, he looked up. In the flare of the torchlight he could see the face of the Indian man.

He spoke, gutturally, but in fair English. "My daughter say you man help her," he said.

"Yes," Rafe replied. "The Sioux are not my enemies, nor am I theirs."

"Your name Caradec." The Indian's statement was flat, not to be contradicted.

"Yes." Rafe stumbled to his feet, rubbing his wrists. "We know your horse, also the horses of the others."

"Others?" Rafe asked quickly. "There are others here?"

"Yes, a girl who rode your horse, and a man who rode one of ours. The man is much better. He had been injured."

Ann and Tex! Rafe's heart leaped.

"May I see them?" he asked. "They are my friends."

The Indian nodded. He studied Rafe for a minute.

"I think you are good man. My name Man Afraid Of His Hoss."

The Ogallala chief!

Rafe looked again at the Indian. "I know the name. With Red Cloud you are the greatest of the Sioux."

The chief nodded. "There are others. John Grass, Gall, Crazy Horse, many others. The Sioux have many great men."

The girl led Rafe away to the tent where he found Tex Brisco lying on a pile of skins and blankets. Tex was pale, but he grinned when Rafe came in.

"Man," he said, "it's good to see you! And here's Ann!"

Rafe turned to look at her. She smiled, then held out her hand.

"I have learned how foolish I was. First from Penn, and then from Mullaney and Tex."

"Penn? Mullaney?" Rafe squinted his eyes. "Are they here?"

Quickly, Ann explained.

"Barkow's dead," Rafe told them. "Shute killed him."

"Ann told me," Tex said. "He had it comin'. Where's Dan Shute now?"

Caradec shrugged. "I don't know, but I'm goin' to find out."

"Please!" Ann came to him. "Don't fight with him, Rafe! There has been enough killing! You might be hurt, and I couldn't stand that."

He looked at her. "Does it matter so much?"

Her eyes fell. "Yes," she said simply, "it does."

Painted Rock lay quiet in a world of white, its shabbiness lost under the purity of freshly fallen snow. Escorted by a band of the Ogallala, Ann, Rafe, and Tex rode to the edge of town, then said a quick good-bye to the friendly warriors.

The street was empty, and the town seemed to have had no word of their coming.

Tex Brisco, still weak and pale from loss of blood, brought up the rear. With Ann, he headed right for the Emporium. Rafe Caradec rode ahead until they neared the National Saloon, then swung to the boardwalk and waited until they had gone by.

Baker came rushing from the store. With Ann's help, he got Tex down and inside.

Rafe Caradec led his own horse down the street and tied it to the hitching rail. Then he glanced up and down the street, looking for Shute. Within a matter of minutes Dan would know he was back. Once he was aware of it there would be trouble.

Pat Higley was inside the store when Rafe entered. He nodded at Rafe's story of what had taken place.

"Shute's been back in town," Higley said. "I reckon

after he lost Ann in the snowstorm he figured she would circle around and come back here."

"Where's Pod Gomer?" Rafe inquired.

"If you mean has he taken out, why I can tell you he hasn't," Baker said. "He's been around with Shute, and he's wearin' double hardware right now."

Higley nodded. "They ain't goin' to give up without a fight," he warned. "They're keepin' some men in town, quite a bunch of 'em."

Rafe also nodded. "That will end as soon as Shute's out of the way."

He looked up as the door pushed open, and started to his feet when Johnny Gill walked in with Rock Mullaney.

"The soldiers rigged a sled," Gill announced at once. "They're takin' Bo back to the Fort, so we reckoned it might be a good idea to come down here and stand by in case of trouble."

Ann came to the door, and stood there watching them. Her eyes continually strayed to Rafe, and he looked up, meeting their glance. Ann flushed and looked away, then invited him to join her for coffee.

Excusing himself, he got up and went inside. Gravely Ann showed him to a chair, brought him a napkin, then poured coffee for him, and put sugar and cream beside his cup. He took the sugar, then looked up at her.

"Can you ever forgive me?" she asked.

"There's nothin' to forgive," he said, "I couldn't blame you. You were sure your father was dead."

"I didn't know why the property should cause all that trouble until I heard of the oil. Is it really worth so much?"

"Quite a lot. Shippin' is the problem now, but that will be taken care of soon, so it could be worth a great deal of money. I expect they knew more about that end of it than we did." Rafe looked up at her. "I never aimed to claim my half of the ranch," he said, "and I don't now. I accepted it just to give me some kind of a legal basis for workin' with you, but now that the trouble is over, I'll give you the deed, the will your father made out, and the other papers."

"Oh, no!" she exclaimed quickly. "You mustn't! I'll need your help to handle things, and you must accept your part of the ranch and stay on. That is," she added, "if you don't think I'm too awful for the way I acted."

He flushed. "I don't think you're awful, Ann," he said clumsily, getting to his feet. "I think you're wonderful. I guess I always have, ever since that first day when I came into the store and saw you."

His eyes strayed and carried their glance out the window. He came to with a start and got to his feet.

"There's Dan Shute," he said. "I've got to go."

Ann arose with him, white to the lips. He avoided her glance, then turned abruptly toward the door. The girl made no protest, but as he started through the curtain, she said, "Come back, Rafe. I'll be waiting!"

He walked to the street door, and the others saw him go, then something in his manner apprised them of what was about to happen. Mullaney caught up his rifle and started for the door also, and Baker reached for a scattergun.

Rafe Caradec glanced quickly up the snow-covered street. One wagon had been down the center of the street about daybreak, and there had been no other traffic except for a few passing riders. Horses stood in front of the National and the Emporium and had kicked up the snow, but otherwise it was an even, unbroken expanse of purest white.

Rafe stepped out on the porch of the Emporium. Dan Shute's gray was tied at the National's hitching rail, but Shute was nowhere in sight. Rafe walked to the corner of the store, his feet crunching on the snow. The sun was coming out, and the snow might soon be gone. As he thought of that, a drop fell from the roof overhead and touched him on the neck.

Dan Shute would be in the National. Rafe walked slowly down the walk to the saloon and pushed open the door. Joe Benson looked up from behind his bar, and hastily moved down toward the other end. Pod Gomer, slumped in a chair at a table across the room, sat up abruptly, his eyes shifting to the big man at the bar.

Dan Shute's back was to the room. In his short, thick coat he looked enormous. His hat was off, and his shock of blond hair, coarse and uncombed, glinted in the sunlight.

Rafe stopped inside the door, his gaze sweeping the room in one all-encompassing glance. Then his eyes riveted on the big man at the bar.

"All right, Shute," he said calmly. "Turn around and take it."

Dan Shute turned and he was grinning. He was grinning widely, but there was a wicked light dancing in his eyes. He stared at Caradec, letting his slow, insolent gaze go over him from head to foot.

"Killin' you would be too easy," he said. "I promised myself that when the time came I would take you apart with my hands, and then if there was anything left, shoot it full of holes. I'm goin' to kill you, Caradec!"

Out of the tail of his eye, Rafe saw that Johnny Gill was leaning against the jamb of the back door, and that Rock Mullaney was just inside of that same door.

"Take off your guns, Caradec, and I'll kill you!" Shute said softly.

"It's their fight," Gill said suddenly. "Let 'em have it the way they want it!"

The voice startled Gomer so that he jerked, and he glanced over his shoulder, his face white. Then the front door pushed open and Higley came in with Baker. Pod Gomer touched his lips with his tongue and shot a sidelong glance at Benson. The saloon-keeper looked unhappy.

Carefully, Dan Shute reached for his belt buckle and

unbuckled the twin belts, laying the big guns on the bar, butts toward him. At the opposite end of the bar, Rafe Caradec did the same. Then, as one man, they shed their coats.

Lithe and broad-shouldered, Rafe was an inch shorter and forty pounds lighter than the other man. Narrow-hipped and lean as a greyhound, he was built for speed, but the powerful shoulders and powerful hands and arms spoke of years of training as well as hard work with a doublejack, ax, or heaving at the heavy, wet lines of a ship.

Dan Shute's neck was thick, his chest broad and massive. His stomach was flat and hard. His hands were big, and he reeked of sheer animal strength and power. Licking his lips like a hungry wolf, he started forward. He was grinning and the light was dancing in his hard gray-white eyes.

He did not rush or leap. He walked right up to Rafe, with that grin on his lips, and Caradec stood flat-footed, waiting for him. But as Shute stepped in close, Rafe suddenly whipped up a left to the wind that beat the man to the punch. Shute winced at the blow and his eyes narrowed. Then he smashed forward with his hard skull, trying for a butt.

Rafe clipped him with an elbow and swung away, keeping out of the corner.

Still grinning, Dan Shute moved in. The big man was deceptively fast. As he moved in, suddenly he jumped and hurled himself feet foremost at Rafe.

Caradec sprang back but too slowly. The legs jack-knifed around his, and Rafe went to the floor! He hit hard, and Dan was the first to move. Throwing himself over he caught his weight on his left hand and swung with his right. It was a wicked, half-arm blow, and it caught Rafe on the chin. Lights exploded in his brain and he felt himself go down.

Rafe rolled his head more by instinct than knowledge

and the blow clipped his ear. He threw his feet high, and tipped Dan over on his head and off his body. Both men came to their feet and hurled themselves at each other with an impact that shook the room.

Rafe's head was roaring. He felt the smashing blows rocking his head from side to side. He smashed an inside right to the face, and saw a thin streak of blood on Shute's cheek. He fired his right down the same groove, and it might as well have been on a track. The split in the skin widened and a trickle of blood started.

Shute took it coming in and never lost stride. He ducked, knocking Rafe off-balance with his shoulder, swinging an overhand punch that caught Rafe on the cheekbone. Rafe tried to sidestep and failed, slipping in a wet spot on the floor. As he went down, Dan Shute aimed a terrific kick at his head that would have ended the fight right there, but Rafe hurled himself at the pivot leg and knocked Dan sprawling.

Both men came up and walked into each other, slugging.

All reason gone, the two men fought like animals, yet worse than animals for in each man was the experience of years of accumulated brawling and slugging in the hard, tough, wild places of the world. They lived by their strength and their hands and the fierce animal drive that was within them, the drive of the fight for survival.

Rafe stepped in, punching Shute with a wicked cutting, stabbing left. And then his right went down the line again and blood streamed from the cut cheek. He shoved Dan back and smashed both hands into the big man's body, then rolled aside and spilled him with a rolling hiplock.

Dan Shute came up, and Rafe walked in. He stabbed a left to the face and Shute's teeth showed through his lip, broken and ugly. Rafe set himself and whipped up an uppercut that stood Shute on his toes.

Tottering and punchdrunk, the light of battle still

flamed in Shute's eyes. He grabbed a bottle and lunged at Rafe, smashing it down on his shoulder. Rafe rolled with the blow and felt the bottle shatter over the end of his shoulder, then he hooked a left with that same numb arm, and felt the fist sink into Shute's body.

Dan Shute hit the table beside which Gene Baker was standing and both went down in a heap. Suddenly, Shute rolled over and came to his knees, his eyes blazing. Blood streamed from the gash in his cheek, open now from mouth to ear, his lips were shreds and a huge blue lump concealed one eye. His face was scarcely human, yet in the remaining eye gleamed a wild, killing, insane light. And in his hands he held Gene Baker's double-barreled shotgun!

He did not speak—just swept the gun up and squeezed down on both triggers!

Yet at the very instant that he squeezed those triggers, Rafe's left hand had dropped to the table near him and with one terrific heave he spun it toward the kneeling man. The gun belched flame and thunder as Rafe hit the floor flat on his stomach and rolled over.

Joe Benson, crouched over the bar, took the full blast of buckshot in the face and went over backward with a queer, choking scream.

Rafe heaved himself erect. Suddenly the room was deathly still. Pod Gomer's face was a blank sheet of white horror as he stared at the spot where Benson had vanished.

Staggering, Caradec walked toward Dan Shute. The man lay on his back, arms outflung, head lying at a queer angle.

Mullaney pointed. "The table!" he said. "It busted his neck!"

Rafe turned and staggered toward the door. Johnny Gill caught him there. He slid an arm under Rafe's shoulders and strapped his guns to his waist.

"What about Gomer?" he asked.

Caradec shook his head. Pod Gomer was getting up to face him, and he lifted a hand.

"Don't start anything. I've had enough. I'll go."

Somebody brought a bucket of water. Rafe fell on his knees and began splashing the ice-cold water over his head and face. When he had dried himself on a towel someone handed him, he started for a coat. Baker had come in with a clean shirt from the store.

"I'm sorry about that shotgun," he said. "It happened so fast I didn't know."

Rafe tried to smile and couldn't. His face was stiff and swollen.

"Forget it," he said. "Let's get out of here."

"You ain't goin' to leave, are you?" Baker asked. "Ann said that she—"

"Leave? Shucks, no! We've got an oil business here, and there's a ranch. While I was at the Fort I had a wire sent to the C Bar down in Texas for some more cattle."

Ann was waiting for him wide-eyed. He walked past her toward the bed and fell across it. "Don't let it get you, honey," he said. "We'll talk about it when I wake up next week!"

She stared at him, started to speak, and a snore sounded in the room.

Ma Baker smiled. "When a man wants to sleep, let him sleep. I'd say he'd earned it!"

Louis L'Amour

THE NUMBER ONE SELLING WESTERN AUTHOR OF ALL TIME. Mr. L'Amour's books have been made into over 25 films including the giant bestseller HONDO. Here is your chance to order any or all direct by mail.

☐	CROSSFIRE TRAIL	13836-4	1.50
☐	HELLER WITH A GUN	13831-3	1.25
☐	HONDO	13830-5	1.50
☐	KILKENNY	13821-6	1.50
☐	LAST STAND AT PAPAGO WELLS	13880-1	1.50
☐	SHOWDOWN AT YELLOW BUTTE	13893-3	1.50
☐	THE TALL STRANGER	13861-5	1.50
☐	TO TAME A LAND	13832-1	1.50
☐	UTAH BLAINE	P3382	1.25

Buy them at your local bookstores or use this handy coupon for ordering:

FAWCETT BOOKS GROUP, 1 Fawcett Place, P.O. Box 1014, Greenwich, Ct. 06830

Please send me the books I have checked above. Orders for less than 5 books must include 60¢ for the first book and 25¢ for each additional book to cover mailing and handling. Postage is FREE for orders of 5 books or more. Check or money order only. Please include sales tax.

Name_____

Address_____

City_____State/Zip_____

Books $ _____
Postage _____
Sales Tax _____
Total $ _____

Please allow 4 to 5 weeks for delivery. This offer expires 10/78.

A-1

WESTERNS

☐	AMBUSH AT JUNCTION ROCK—MacLeod	P3471	1.25
☐	THE APACHE HUNTER—Shirreffs	P3479	1.25
☐	BARREN LAND SHOWDOWN—Short	13659-0	1.25
☐	BOWMAN'S KID—Shirreffs	13599-3	1.25
☐	CHARRO!—Whittington	13703-1	1.25
☐	CIMARRON JORDAN—Braun	P3201	1.25
☐	DAKOTA BOOMTOWN—Castle	P3521	1.25
☐	DAY OF THE BUZZARD—Olsen	P3530	1.25
☐	THE EASY GUN—Parsons	13712-0	1.25
☐	GRINGO—Foreman	13555-1	1.25
☐	THE GUNSHARP—Cox	13549-7	1.25
☐	HE RODE ALONE—Frazee	13581-0	1.25
☐	THE KID FROM RINCON—Moore	13612-4	1.25
☐	KING FISHER'S ROAD—Rifkin	13711-2	1.25
☐	A MAN NAMED YUMA—Olsen	13616-7	1.25
☐	THE MANHUNTER—Shirreffs	13728-7	1.25
☐	THE MARAUDERS—Shirreffs	13723-6	1.50
☐	SMOKY VALLEY—Hamilton	13677-9	1.50
☐	TO HELL AND TEXAS—Lutz	13597-7	1.25
☐	TOP MAN WITH A GUN—Patten	13705-8	1.25
☐	WHITE APACHE—Forrest	13754-6	1.25

Buy them at your local bookstores or use this handy coupon for ordering:

FAWCETT BOOKS GROUP, 1 Fawcett Place, P.O. Box 1014, Greenwich, Ct.06830

Please send me the books I have checked above. Orders for less than 5 books must include 60¢ for the first book and 25¢ for each additional book to cover mailing and handling. Postage is FREE for orders of 5 books or more. Check or money order only. Please include sales tax.

Name_____

Address_____

City_____State/Zip_____

Books $_____
Postage   _____
Sales Tax   _____
Total $_____

Please allow 4 to 5 weeks for delivery. This offer expires 10/78.

A-4

BESTSELLERS